KT-378-954

Cast of Characters

Kate Rebel: Matriarch of the Rebel family.

Falcon: The oldest son—the strong one. Reunited with his wife, Leah, and proud father of Eden and John.

Egan: The loner. Married to Rachel Hollister, daughter of the man who put him in jail.

Quincy: The peacemaker. Married to Jenny Walker, his childhood best friend.

Elias: The fighter. Falls in love with the archenemy of the family's daughter.

Paxton: The lover. Never met a woman he couldn't have, but the woman he wants doesn't want him.

Jude: The serious, responsible one. Raising his small son alone.

Phoenix: The wild one and the youngest. He's wild and free until Child Protective Services says he's the father of a small boy.

Abraham (Abe) Rebel: Paternal grandfather.

Jericho Johnson: Egan's friend from prison.

Texas Rebels: Jude

LINDA WARREN

ST. HELENS
COMMUNITY
LIBRARIES

ACC No   F16

CLASS No

MILLS & BOON

All rights reserved including the right of reproduction
in whole or in part in any form. This edition is published
by arrangement with Harlequin Books S.A.

This is a work of fiction. Names, characters, places,
locations and incidents are purely fictional and bear
no relationship to any real life individuals, living or
dead, or to any actual places, business establishments,
locations, events or incidents. Any resemblance is
entirely coincidental.

This book is sold subject to the condition that it shall
not, by way of trade or otherwise, be lent, resold, hired
out or otherwise circulated without the prior consent
of the publisher in any form of binding or cover other
than that in which it is published and without a similar
condition including this condition being imposed on the
subsequent purchaser.

® and TM are trademarks owned and used by the
trademark owner and/or its licensee. Trademarks
marked with ® are registered with the United Kingdom
Patent Office and/or the Office for Harmonisation in the
Internal Market and in other countries.

First Published in Great Britain 2016
By Mills & Boon, an imprint of HarperCollins*Publishers*
1 London Bridge Street, London, SE1 9GF

Large Print edition 2016

© 2016 Linda Warren

ISBN: 978-0-263-06607-4

Our policy is to use papers that are natural, renewable
and recyclable products and made from wood grown
in sustainable forests. The logging and manufacturing
processes conform to the legal environmental
regulations of the country of origin.

Printed and bound in Great Britain
by CPI Antony Rowe, Chippenham, Wiltshire

A two-time RITA® Award–nominated author, **Linda Warren** has written thirty-eight books and has received the Readers' Choice Award, the Holt Medallion, the Booksellers' Best Award, the Book Buyers Best Award, the Golden Quill and RT Reviewers' Choice Best Book Award. A native Texan, she is a member of Romance Writers of America and the West Houston chapter. She lives in College Station with her husband and a menagerie of animals, including a Canada goose named Broken Wing. You can learn more about Linda and her books at lindawarren.net.

Acknowledgments

A special thanks to Scott Conoly, MD, for graciously sharing his knowledge of medical school.

And thanks to Jenny Ferro Siegert for discussing courses and timeline for premed students.

Also, thanks to Crystal Breihan Siegert for taking time to answer questions about gifted children.

All errors are strictly mine.

Dedication

To my brother, Paul William, who generated laughter in all of us.

Prologue

My name is Kate Rebel. I married John Rebel when I was eighteen years old and then bore him seven sons. We worked the family ranch, which John later inherited. We put everything we had into buying more land so our sons would have a legacy. We didn't have much, but we had love.

The McCray Ranch borders Rebel Ranch on the east and the McCrays have forever been a thorn in my family's side. They've cut our fences, dammed up creeks to limit our water supply and shot one of our prize bulls. Ezra McCray threatened to shoot our sons if he caught them jumping his fences again. We tried to keep our boys away, but they are boys—young and wild.

One day Jude and Phoenix, two of our youngest, were out riding together. When John heard shots, he immediately went to find his boys. They lay on the ground, blood oozing from their heads. Ezra McCray was astride a horse twenty yards away with a rifle in his hand. John drew his gun and fired, killing Ezra instantly. Both boys survived with only minor wounds. Since my husband was protecting his children, he didn't spend even one night in jail. This escalated the feud that still goes on today.

The man I knew as my husband died that day. He couldn't live with what he'd done, and started to drink heavily. I had to take over the ranch and the raising of our boys. John died ten years later. We've all been affected by the tragedy, especially my sons.

They are grown men now and deal in different ways with the pain of losing their father. One day I pray my boys will be able to put this behind them and live healthy, normal lives with women who will love them the way I loved their father.

Chapter One

Jude: the sixth son—the quiet one

A cowboy's broken heart.

They could say a lot of things about Jude Rebel, but they couldn't say he wasn't a good father.

He'd devoted his life to Zane.

But tonight for the first time in twelve years he was going out on a date. He swiped an electric razor lightly over his jawline, leaving a bit of scruff. Women liked an outdoorsy look, he'd been told. In reality he had no idea what women liked. Ever since the day Paige

Wheeler had told him, "I'm pregnant," his fascination with the opposite sex had come to a screeching halt.

Paige. They'd discovered sex together and to him it was better than sneaking a beer with the guys or riding his horse or swimming in Yaupon Creek. It was better than anything he'd ever experienced in his life. Every spare moment, he'd spent with her, and they'd been inseparable. Until…

He shoved the memory back in place, tucked away in a dark corner of his mind. Never Never Land, he called it. A place he never wanted to visit again.

His phone lay on the bathroom vanity and he tapped it just to reread her message.

Tonight at seven. Can't wait.

Annabel Hurley—blonde, twenty-five and about the prettiest thing he'd seen in a long time—had asked him to dinner. She was one of Zane's teachers and they'd spent a lot of time together in the past year trying to figure out ways to keep Zane interested in school other than letting him play video games non-stop. His son was gifted and in the Pre-Advanced Placement program. He was still bored in class because he always completed his assignments before the other kids. Not wanting to move him up a grade for a second time, Jude searched for other answers. Annabel had been a godsend. She was so patient with Zane.

Going out with Annabel was his first step in putting Never Never Land behind him and not having to shove it to the back of his mind to keep from enduring the pain.

Jude had a day of work ahead of him and then he was going to get back in the game of living and experiencing life again. He walked into the bedroom and grabbed a T-shirt from a drawer and pulled it over his head. Shoving his arms into a Western shirt, he thought about Annabel. He liked her and enjoyed her company. He'd have to be dead from the waist down not to.

As he sat on the bed to put on his boots, his eye caught the photo on his nightstand. He picked it up. It was a photo of him holding Zane on the day after he was born. Jude looked so young and scared cradling the tiny baby wrapped in a blue blanket. All the fear of that day showed in the sad darkness of his eyes. Memories floated across his mind like gray thunderclouds about to dump a lot more tears on him.

What are we going to do, Jude? We don't know anything about babies.

Jude hadn't had an answer. He'd been shell-shocked and was trying to grasp what this meant for their future. So they'd done what naive, scared teenagers do: they ignored the problem in hopes it would go away. It didn't.

Paige started to show, but she'd never been

slim and wore big bulky blouses so no one could tell she was pregnant. But he knew. They would sit in his truck while Paige talked about what they needed to do. Jude listened. But he never said anything.

I've been talking to the school counselor and I told her about the baby. She knows about my premed scholarship to Berkeley and how I dreamed of this for years. She said I had choices and I should consider them.

Choices? To him there were no choices. Just one—the baby was theirs and they had to raise it. But he never said so.

Of course, abortion is out of the question. The counselor said adoption might be an option for us. She knows a couple who wants a baby. They're educated and have a nice home and they would love and care for our baby, something that we can't do.

Why not? They were young, but his brother

had raised his daughter on his own, so why couldn't Jude? But he never said so.

We have to make a decision, Jude. We have to do something. The baby's due in August and we graduate in May. What do you think?

He'd shrugged.

You always do that. You never say anything and that makes me so mad. This is your baby, too. What should we do?

They were sitting in his truck at the high school and he stared out to the vacant parking lot. He knew what he would do, but so many things kept him silent. Paige had had an awful childhood and her dream was to get out of Horseshoe and live a better life. Her mother was an alcoholic and spent most of her time down at Rowdy's Beer Joint drinking and picking up strange men.

Many a night Paige would call Jude and he would go pick her up because she was scared of the men her mother brought home. One night a man had come into her room and she'd run outside and slept in the yard. Ever since then she'd been afraid when her mom had a man friend over. No one should have to live like that. Especially someone as sweet and gentle as Paige.

"Can you give up our child?" was the only thing he could say.

"I don't know." She started to cry and he took her in his arms and told her that whatever she wanted to do, he would be okay with it. He never said what he really thought.

Paige took care of everything and the adoption was set up. Jude hated the whole thing and he tried not to think about it. As August drew near, Paige gained a lot of weight all over and no one, not even her mother or sister, suspected she was pregnant. And everyone in Horseshoe knew Paige ate when her mom was on one of her drinking binges.

A week before the due date Jude told his

mother he was taking a few days off to get away with his friends. Instead he picked up Paige and they drove to a clinic in Austin, one the adoptive parents had chosen, to have the baby. They would induce labor so Paige could have the baby early and continue on with her plans to go to California.

Not a lot was said on the drive. Paige had made up her mind and Jude wanted her to have her dream. She deserved better than the life she had and he didn't want to take that away from her.

They went into an office and signed papers. They would sign the adoption papers after the birth. The adoptive parents' lawyer had set everything up. Jude and Paige would never meet them, nor would they see their child. Jude's hand shook as he wrote his name and he fought tears that stung the backs of his eyes. But he was a Rebel and he wouldn't cry.

They hugged tightly and Paige was taken to

an operating room. He waited. And waited. He wanted to talk to his brother Quincy to tell him what was going on, but Quincy was in the army and stationed in Afghanistan. And he couldn't heap another burden on his mother. He had to endure this alone.

It was hours later when the nurse came out and told him the baby had been born and he could see Paige. They had been asked if they wanted to see the baby and the counselor had advised against it. And against knowing the sex. It was best to make a clean break, she'd said. They would never know if they had a boy or a girl. Paige had listened to everything the woman had said and Jude had felt powerless.

Paige lay in a bed, pale and crying. That shook him. He sat by her bed, holding her hand as she continued to cry. They didn't say anything. Words now were useless. That night he slept in his truck and the next day, after they signed the adoption papers, he drove Paige back to Horseshoe.

She had her things packed and they loaded them into his truck and drove away. Paige had already said goodbye to her sister, so she didn't look back. There was nothing left for her in the small town where she'd grown up. Not even Jude.

Paige cried all the way to the airport. Being young and scared himself, he had no idea how to comfort her. They'd made a decision and now they had to live with it. As he stopped at the terminal, she leaned over and hugged him and whispered, "I'm sorry." Then she grabbed her bags from the backseat and ran into the airport. He never heard from her or saw her again.

Placing the photo back on his nightstand, he drew a heavy breath. On the way to the ranch Jude kept thinking, *I gave my child away.* The closer he got to home, the more those words hurt and the more he thought about his father, who had told him in the girls/sex speech to always take responsibility. *Be a man. Be a Rebel. A Rebel never shirks his responsibility and I expect my boys to never let me down in that respect.*

He'd let his father down. He'd given away his child.

By the time he crossed the cattle guard to Rebel Ranch, he knew he couldn't live with that decision. He'd thought he could, but he soon found that blood was thicker than any commitment he'd made to Paige.

He drove to the barn looking for Falcon in hopes that he could help him decide what to do. But Falcon and four of his other brothers were working on the ranch. His mom's truck was at the house and he quickly drove there. He had to tell her, even though he'd rather take a beating than see the look of disappointment on her face.

She was in the kitchen fixing supper and he

would always remember the smell of chicken-fried steak wafting to him as he talked and told her where he'd been and what he'd done.

Her response was unusual. "Have you been drinking, Jude? If this was Phoenix, I would know it was a joke. But you…"

He was known for his quietness and his responsible behavior, so it was a shock to his mom.

"No, Mom. I need your help. I can't let them keep my child."

She removed her apron and slammed it onto the counter. "I'll get my purse." And then they were on their way back to Austin. His mom called her brother, Gabe, who was interning in a law firm, and he met them there.

They asked to speak with the administrator of the hospital and he told them that the adoptive parents were already with the baby. He suggested that Jude think about his decision a little more. His child would have a mother and a father, something he couldn't give it.

Jude stood on shaky legs and looked the man square in the eye. "I want my kid." This time he said it out loud.

It was a private adoption, so the administrator called the attorney handling the case. Once he arrived, Gabe asked to see the contract Jude had signed. It clearly stated that the parents, Jude Rebel and Paige Wheeler, had ten days to change their minds. The man then said they would need Paige's consent. Gabe pointed out the contract didn't say that, and he warned that if the baby wasn't brought to them soon, he would call the authorities.

The attorney and Gabe continued to argue about Jude's rights. Jude was sick to his stomach and had to go to the bathroom to throw up. His nerves were about to get the best of him. As he came out of the bathroom, he saw Mrs. Nancy Carstairs, the counselor who had advised Paige, standing at the end of the hall. That threw him. He didn't understand what she was doing at the hospital.

He went back to Gabe and mentioned it to him. Gabe flipped through some papers he'd gotten from the adoption attorney and gave him the answer: Tom and Nancy Carstairs were the adoptive parents.

Rage filled Jude. Mrs. Carstairs had given Paige advice that would make it easier to adopt their baby. She'd continued to feed her bad information to make sure Paige gave away their child. He stomped down the hall to Mrs. Carstairs and he lost his cool for the first time in his life. Gabe had to pull him away and his mom had to calm him down. He wanted to strangle the woman for what she'd done to their lives.

Gabe told the attorney and the administrator if the baby wasn't brought to them immediately, he would file charges against Nancy

Carstairs for coercing Paige Wheeler into giving away her child. And he would notify the school board in Horseshoe of her deceit. And he would also bring charges against the hospital.

The Carstairs caved and walked out of the facility. The nurse in charge of the newborns said she would bring the baby, but not until Jude had a proper car seat and items to care for his child.

His mother went shopping while he and Gabe waited. It was the longest wait of his life. His mother had come back by the time the doors opened and the nurse came out carrying a baby wrapped in a blue blanket. *He had a son.* His breath caught and it took a moment before he could breathe again. He had a son.

The days that followed weren't easy. He learned to change diapers, prepare bottles and wake at the smallest of cries. He followed his brother Falcon's example and raised his kid—

because that was what fathers did. And no one was ever going to take his child again. Because he'd said so.

"Dad." Zane ran through the bathroom they shared into Jude's room. "The entry form for the race is supposed to be in today's paper. If Uncle Falcon doesn't bring it in, can I take your truck and go get it at the mailbox?"

His son loved horses and he was planning to enter the Horseshoe Founder's Day Horse Race at the end of April. That was all that was on his mind.

Jude got to his feet and stuffed his shirt into his jeans. "I'll get it." He looked at his son standing there in nothing but his boxer shorts. His dark hair fell into his eyes and he brushed it aside, as he often did. All arms and legs, he was going to be a gangly teenager just like Jude. His dark eyes and facial features were all Jude, too. But his sweet nature, which endeared him to everyone, he got from his mother. "Get dressed. It's time for breakfast."

"Okay, Dad." Zane dashed toward the bathroom. "Don't forget about the form."

As if Jude could forget. Zane had talked about the race nonstop since before Christmas and he'd been practicing with his paint horse, Running Bear, almost every day. Jude felt sure there wasn't a horse in the county that could beat him.

He made his way down the stairs to the kitchen, where his mom was cooking breakfast. The smell of bacon frying whet his appetite. He didn't know how he would've raised Zane if it hadn't been for his mom. She didn't criticize or judge him. She just pitched in and helped him and showed him how to be a father. The only drawback was he was thirty-one years old and still living with his mother. That, he could handle. Not having his son with him was something he couldn't.

"Mornin', Mom," he said, snatching a piece of bacon before pouring a cup of coffee.

She turned from the stove. "Mornin', son. Is Zane up?"

"Yes, and I didn't even have to wake him. He's so excited about this race that it's all he thinks about, even in his sleep." He took a couple of sips of coffee and placed his cup on the counter. "I'm going to the mailbox to get the paper so he can have the form to fill out or he's going to drive us all crazy."

Before he could get to the door, Falcon and Quincy, two of his brothers, came in. Quincy had the paper in his hand. He held it up. "I brought something for Zane. Is he up?"

Jude picked up his cup. "Yes, and he's ready for that form. He's saved up the entry fee and he's counting the days. Actually, he has a calendar in his room and he's marking them off."

"Who wants breakfast?" his mom asked.

"I had breakfast with Leah," Falcon replied. "Our children were asleep and it was nice."

"How about you, Quincy?"

"Elias had a late night, so I fixed breakfast for Grandpa." Quincy filled a cup with coffee and sat at the table.

"Your grandpa can come over here and eat if he wants breakfast," their mom snapped in a tone they knew well. "You have a wife and you need to be home with her and not pampering that old man." His mom and grandfather had a strained relationship that was difficult for the whole family.

Quincy stretched his shoulders. "Mom, my wife was up at 5:00 a.m. to be at work at six. We had coffee and went our separate ways. But we took time for ourselves, if you know what I mean."

"Quincy," his mother scolded. But Quincy only smiled. It was good to see his brother happy.

Jude filled his plate with bacon, eggs and biscuits and sat at the table.

Falcon flipped through the hometown paper, which usually had nothing in it but tidbits of gossip. Nothing ever happened in Horseshoe, Texas. But Falcon slid the paper over to Jude, pointing to a page.

Jude took a swallow of coffee, pushed his plate away and picked up the paper. The headline hit him between the eyes like a two-by-four.

Hometown Girl Made Good Returns.

Jude quickly scanned the rest of the story. Paige's mother had died and she was coming home for the funeral. Oh, man. He'd never expected this. Darlene Wheeler had fallen and broken her hip not long after Paige had left for California. Her daughter Staci had put her in a rehab center in Austin and from there she'd been moved to a nursing facility. That was the gossip Jude had heard.

A knot the size of a baseball formed in his stomach.

Never Never Land leaped to the forefront of his mind. The Wheelers still owned a house in Horseshoe and Staci paid the taxes on it. Jude wasn't sure why they'd never sold it. Twelve years had come full circle and it was time to tell Paige what he'd done.

That was his first thought.

The second was there was no way in hell. Zane was his and he had to think about his son now. About what this would do to him. Jude had always told him the truth. Zane was about five when he'd first asked about his mother. He wanted to know why he didn't have one. He almost thought that was normal since his cousin Eden hadn't had one, either. But Zane was smart and he soon realized that most of his friends had mothers.

At that time Jude had glossed over most of the story and said Zane's mother had wanted to further her education and had left for college.

As he grew older, Zane asked more questions and Jude decided then not to lie to him, because he knew his father would never have lied to him. Again, he told him how young they'd been and how they hadn't known anything about babies and they had decided to give him up for adoption so he could have a good life. Jude tried to sound matter-of-fact about what had happened, but Zane knew his mother had given him away.

He glanced at the paper one more time. Paige was returning to Horseshoe. How did he tell her what he'd done?

Or did he need to?

She'd made her choice and he'd made his.

But… That *but* carried a whole lot of guilt that was gnawing away at his insides.

Paige Wheeler, Zane's mother, would be back in Horseshoe.

Soon.

The knot tightened.

Chapter Two

Nausea churned in Paige's stomach as the plane touched down in Austin, Texas. She took several deep breaths to calm herself. She'd never expected going home would make her sick.

"Are you all right, dear?" the elderly woman next to her asked.

Paige took another deep breath. "Yes, I guess I'm just a little nervous."

"I was like that the first time I flew, but you get used to it."

Paige smiled patiently at the woman, not wanting to explain her nervous stomach had nothing to do with flying. It had to do with facing her past and all the mistakes she'd made. Actually, just one mistake. The big one that haunted her days and nights.

Passengers began to stand and Paige reached for her carryall to join the queue leaving the plane. She navigated the airport and quickly made it to the baggage carousel to retrieve her luggage. Holding her suitcase, she looked around for her sister and saw her across the room, waving.

Time stood still for a moment as she gazed at the sister who had been a lifeline. Staci was two years older and had taken care of Paige, especially when their mother was on one of her rampages. And that had been quite often when she'd been drinking. Their mother had blamed them for her lousy life and she'd taken it out on them whenever she could.

She'd never hit them. That would have left bruises. She'd used words that left scars buried deep inside, scars that would never heal.

Their brother, Luke, had joined the army right out of high school and that had left Staci and Paige to fend for themselves.

There'd always been men in their mother's life. The three of them all had different fathers, whose identities were a mystery to them and surely to their mother, too. Paige used to search the faces of men in town trying to find a resemblance, but she'd soon given up, knowing it wouldn't make any difference. But she would always wonder. That was just human nature.

A lousy childhood had not prepared her for the real world. Her dream was to leave Horseshoe and to get as far away from her mother as she could. That was why she'd studied constantly and gotten good grades—to win a scholarship so she could get out of a home life where she was criticized and demeaned.

Her ticket out had come with a price. One she'd thought she could pay, but she'd been wrong. The price was too high. A naive, troubled girl didn't realize it at the time. And she would pay that price for the rest of her life.

She walked toward her sister, carrying her luggage. Staci looked much the same, only older. They'd once had the same mousy-brown hair, as her mother had called it. When Paige was little, she thought she had mice in her hair. She hadn't quite understood the description. When she was older, she knew it was just one more criticism her mother had heaped upon her.

Other than that, they didn't resemble each other. And their looks had changed some over the years. With the help of a good stylist, Staci's hair was now a darker brown, which looked great with her blue eyes. Paige had trimmed and highlighted her thick tresses so she was now more of a blonde with dark green eyes. Their brother had brown eyes. They were an eclectic mix or a hodgepodge of their mother's love life.

Paige dropped her suitcase and hugged her sister tightly. She'd missed her. But not as much as she'd missed… She couldn't think his name. She just couldn't. Or the nausea would come back.

Staci drew back and looked at her sister. "My, look at you. Don't you look sophisticated in heels and a nice dress. I love your hair! California has changed you, or has being a doctor made this transformation?"

"Me?" Paige quickly steered the conversation in another direction. "Look at you! How much weight have you lost?" Both sisters had a tendency to gain weight. They had that in common.

"About thirty pounds." Staci swung around in her summer dress and did a bow. "I feel great. I have a fabulous job and great friends and I feel good about myself for the first time in my life."

"It shows." Staci had a job at a hotel in Austin. She'd started working at a hotel in Temple right out of high school and was soon offered a better job with more benefits in Austin. She was in charge of parties and banquets and she loved it.

Nothing else was said as they made their way to Staci's car and it gave Paige a chance to re-group and calm her shaky nerves. She'd talked to her sister many times over the years, but she never shared her deep dark secrets with any-one, not even her sister. The embarrassment and shame she couldn't share. It went deep into her soul where no one was allowed. She'd been a private person all her life and the only one she'd let get close was...

"Have you heard from Luke?" Paige asked to change her train of thought.

"Yes. He'll be at the funeral tomorrow. He's stationed at Fort Polk and he'll be leaving at the end of the month for another deployment."

"I know. We spoke last week." They reached

the car and Paige put her suitcase in the backseat and got in the vehicle. "I'm so proud of
him and what he's accomplished with his career in the army."

Staci backed out of the parking spot and
headed for the exit sign. "I'm proud of all of
us. After a traumatic childhood, we turned out
pretty good."

Paige smoothed the fabric of her dress and
then watched as the parking terminal flashed
by. "Do you think any of us will ever be happy,
though?"

"I'm happy," Staci insisted. "I meet so many
wonderful people and they're kind and gra-
cious and treat me with respect. That's all a
person needs."

"And love," Paige murmured under her
breath.

"Well—" Staci turned out of the terminal
"—we're kind of gun-shy in that department,

but you know what love is. And one time you were madly in love with—"

"Don't say his name." Paige stopped her with panic in her voice.

Staci gave her a sharp glance as she negotiated the traffic. "Why not? It was a long time ago and you've both moved on. He has a little boy now. I haven't been back to Horseshoe all that much, so I don't know the details about his marriage."

He'd married someone else. He had a child. While she…

"Could we not talk about it, please?"

"Okay." They drove in silence for a long time before Staci said, "What's going on with you? You're tense and sad and it's not about Mom's death."

Paige swallowed the lump in her throat. "It's very upsetting to go back and relive all that heartache and pain."

"Yeah, I know, kiddo. I lived through it with

you. But as I told you on the phone a couple years ago, the doctors at the mental hospital said Mom's problems started with the wreck that killed her parents. She suffered severe head trauma and back injuries, and she wasn't the same afterward. Even Uncle Harry said that. As the years passed, it just got worse because she refused any treatment and couldn't stay off the liquor."

Paige had always known there had to be a reason for her mother's behavior, but it still didn't wipe away a child's pain. Her mother was gone now and she had to learn to forgive. She knew all too well how circumstances could change a person's life.

"How often did you visit her?"

Staci heaved a sigh. "Whenever I could force myself to go—holidays, her birthday and Mother's Day. I always took her flowers and chocolates. At the end, she was very sad, Paige."

She closed her eyes tightly, not wanting to hear any good things about her mother. In her emotional state, she couldn't handle it. The bitterness and the resentment held her together like Elmer's glue, and if they were gone, she would crumble into nothing. Her sins would rise to the surface and she would have to admit that she was worse than her mother. At least her mother had never given away one of her children.

"Enough with the maudlin stuff. I have a two-bedroom apartment and you and Luke are staying with me. I thought it would be nice if we were together. He's coming in tonight and we'll have dinner. I'm cooking. And it's not peanut butter and jelly or corn dogs. How did we survive on that?"

"Don't forget milk and cereal."

"Mmm. But, you know, the past is the past and what we do now with our lives is up to us.

Adversity has made us stronger and we can handle anything."

Paige wasn't so sure about that. She didn't know if she could handle going back to Horseshoe, Texas, and reliving that terrible time.

JUDE RODE INTO the barn followed by his brother Phoenix. He was home from the rodeo circuit for a few days and helping on the ranch. He and Phoenix had been born in the same year, January and December, and they were close growing up, almost like twins. But Phoenix had always had an interest in the rodeo, while Jude had just wanted to cowboy for real.

As they were unsaddling, Quincy and Elias rode in from their day's work on the ranch. "I'll finish up for you, Jude," Quincy said. "You got a date tonight and it's getting late."

Jude threw his saddle over a rail. "I canceled."

His brothers stopped what they were doing

and stared at him. Quincy placed his hands on his hips. "Why?"

"I can't go out and have a good time with this Paige thing hanging over my head. I have to figure out what I'm going to do. I have to think about Zane and what's best for him."

Elias pulled off his hat, slapped it against his leg, making the dust fly. "The way I see it, Paige is here for a funeral, and as soon as it's over, she'll be gone again. She probably has a big practice out in California. I don't know what you're worried about."

"I usually never agree with Elias, but he could be right." Quincy hung his saddle on a rail and stared at Jude. "Go out and have a good time tonight and you'll be relaxed and able to see things more clearly."

"You wouldn't do that, Quincy. You wouldn't put your pleasure before someone you loved."

Quincy pulled off his gloves and stuffed

them into his saddlebags. "Yeah, you're probably right."

"Paige is Zane's mother and I have to tell her what I did or I'll never be able to live with myself. Doesn't matter if she's married and has other kids. Zane has a right to know his mother and maybe get the chance to meet her."

All day, thoughts of Zane and Paige had gone round and round in his mind. It all came down to the same thing: what was best for Zane. Jude had lived his whole life with that in mind and he wasn't changing now, even if it was going to take a piece of his heart to face her.

Falcon walked into the barn. "Everybody through for the day?"

"Yeah," Quincy replied. "We have twenty-five heifers ready to go first thing in the morning to Mr. Hensley in Longview, Texas. Actually, we have twenty-six." He glanced at Elias. "Someone can't count."

"Math wasn't my strong suit." Elias smirked.

Falcon pointed a finger at Elias. "First thing in the morning before anyone goes to work, you'll get that heifer back to the herd."

"You're a hard-ass, Falcon. Why don't you just ask Mr. Hensley if he would like twenty-six? Maybe give them a discounted rate."

"I'm not discounting those heifers. They're prime stock and it's how we make our living. Have you forgotten that?"

Jericho, who worked on the ranch and was a friend of their brother Egan, came into the barn from the corral. "Don't worry about the extra heifer. I let one of the smaller ones out into the alley that connects most of the pastures and she took off running. I followed her on my horse all the way to the north pasture. She's now back with the herd."

Elias thumbed his nose at Falcon. "And that's how it's done, big brother."

Falcon shook his head and caught sight of

Jude. "What are you still doing here? I thought you had a date tonight."

Phoenix held up his hands. "Okay, everybody, leave Jude alone. This is his decision, his kid, not yours."

Jude and Phoenix had shared a special connection ever since the shooting of Ezra McCray. Jude and Phoenix had been riding bareback while their father was fixing fences. Jude was in front and Phoenix sat behind him with his arms wrapped around Jude's waist. Almost as if it were yesterday, Jude could hear his brother.

Jump the fence, Jude. This horse can do it.

We'll get in trouble.

Dad's way over there and we'll be back before he misses us. Jump the fence, Jude.

Hold on, he said and kneed the horse.

The horse shot forward, galloping faster and faster as it neared the fence and they sailed right over it, but Jude couldn't stop the horse fast enough. Before he could turn back toward the fence, shots rang out and the next thing he knew, he was in a hospital bed with his mother crying and his dad looking as if the world had come to an end. His sun-browned face was a mask of pain, misery and suffering. At six years of age, Jude thought maybe Phoenix was dead and he started to cry, too. But he soon found out Phoenix was fine and that Ezra McCray had shot at them. And his father had killed the man. It was a lot for a six-year-old to understand. It was a lot for a six-year-old to go through.

From that day forward, Jude never spoke much. He was quiet and stayed close to his father, but even at that early age, he could see his dad was troubled by what had happened. Jude blamed himself and tried to make his father feel better. All his life he seemed to be fighting to make someone feel better and he had grown weary of the task.

"Why didn't Paxton come home with you?" Falcon asked Phoenix, his voice piercing Jude's troubled thoughts.

"He went on to another rodeo with Cole Bryant. He's focused and determined to stay on the top of his game so he can make the national finals in Vegas. He'll be home in a few days."

Paxton had had a rough year. He'd dumped his high-school sweetheart, Jenny, for someone he'd met at a rodeo and it had turned out to be a nightmare for him. It had almost done him in, especially since Jenny had fallen in love with Quincy and they were now married. The brothers had worked everything out, and Paxton wasn't letting anything or anyone interfere with his career again.

"Has anyone heard from Egan?" Falcon was doing his usual thing, keeping tabs on the brothers.

"No," Jericho said. "They're supposed to find out the sex of the baby today, but Egan wants to wait until the birth. If I was a betting man, and I gave that up a long time ago, I'd bet they're going to wait."

Jericho was one of a kind. He'd grown up on the streets of Houston, wrapped up with gangs and drugs. Egan had met him in prison, when he'd been unjustly sent there by an overzealous judge. Jericho had saved his life and Egan was forever indebted to him. When the family got Egan out, their mother promised Jericho a job for his bravery.

The man stood about six feet four inches tall. He had dark features with a scar slashed across the side of his face. His long dark hair was tied into a ponytail at his neck. No one knew his lineage, but Egan had said he was part white, black, Mexican and Indian. A scary figure to some, but to the Rebel family he was loved and trusted.

"Leah and I waited," Falcon said. "Of course, ours was a completely different situation, but

I agree with Jericho. Egan will win this round because Rachel will do what he wants."

"You guys are pathetic." Elias laughed. "Why doesn't he just say no?"

"If you ever find anyone to marry you, we'll remind you of that," Falcon told him, and looked around. "Where's Grandpa?"

"He was right behind me." Elias walked to the barn door and looked out. "Can you believe this? His horse is tied to the chain-link fence at his house. Who does he think is going to un-saddle that horse and take care of it?"

Elias's cell phone buzzed before anyone could answer.

"That's probably him about to tell you," Phoenix said.

Elias fished his cell out of his pocket and frowned. "It's Grandpa. Thank you, Quincy, for buying him a phone." Elias clicked it on. "Yeah, Grandpa. I'll do it. What did you say?" Elias pushed Speakerphone and held the cell up. "You're my favorite grandson," echoed through the barn and everyone tried hard not to laugh. It was Grandpa's favorite saying, and he'd said it to every one of the brothers at some point.

Elias slipped the phone back into his pocket. "The favorite grandson is going to go help his grandpa. Now don't y'all feel guilty?"

Quincy's cell buzzed and he quickly grabbed it from his pocket. After a second, he said, "I got to go. That was Jenny. White Dove is in labor. Jenny has been watching that horse for days and I hope everything goes okay." He hurried toward the barn door and then turned back. "Jude, Zane wanted to be there. Do you want me to call him?"

"Go ahead." He threw a blanket over the saddle. "It would give him something to do while I'm out. I'm going into town to see Annabel. She deserves an explanation."

"Good for you." Quincy hurried away and

Falcon and Jericho soon followed. That left him and Phoenix to sort through the tangled mess of Jude's mind.

"You okay?" Phoenix asked.

Jude leaned against the railing. "Do you feel you will never be the same as you were when you were five years old?"

"Come on, Jude." Phoenix shoved his hands into the front pockets of his jeans as if that could keep the memories at bay. "This family will never be the same, but we have to learn to accept happiness and forgiveness into our lives. I'm doing that. Dad said it wasn't our fault and I believe him because I believed him all my life and I'm not going to change now. We were kids and kids do silly things. We're not to blame. Dad said so."

"It's just…"

"What is it with you and Quincy? You both seem to have a need to carry the weight of the world on your shoulders. Let it go. Please."

"Dad was gone two years when Paige got pregnant and I needed to talk to him so badly. Quincy was in the army and I couldn't talk to him, either. I made all the wrong decisions and I can't even say it was for the right reasons. I was just a scared kid and I didn't know what to do. I just wanted Paige to get out of a bad home life and the scholarship gave her that opportunity. I couldn't take that away from her."

"Jude, you did the right thing. You went back and got your son and he's an amazing kid. Pat yourself on the back for once. If you feel you have to tell Paige, then tell her. Zane is a different matter. But I'm sure you'll make the right decision for him, too. Stop agonizing over it." He grabbed the reins of Jude's horse. "Go spend some time with that pretty teacher and I'll take care of the horses. And, for heaven sakes, smile, Jude. You're freaking me out."

"I just don't want to hurt her."

The horses milled around, neighing, ready for feed.

"Well, I'm not judging her or anything, but I can almost guarantee you before this is over, someone is going to get hurt and I'm just hoping it's not you or Zane. Just saying."

Phoenix was right. He couldn't make any of this better for any of them. He just had to make sure his son wasn't hurt. While Paige was in town, he somehow had to explain what had happened all those years ago. She deserved that. He knew that with all his heart and nothing anyone said would change his mind. Sometimes in life he had to make the rough decisions because he was a father. He could only pray this decision was the right one for his son.

And Paige.

Chapter Three

"Dad, Dad…"

Jude sat up in bed and squinted at the clock. Five in the morning. "What are you doing up so early?"

Zane jerked on his jeans. "I want to go check on the new foal. It was amazing, Dad. White Dove was nervous and Uncle Quincy just talked to her and rubbed her head and her stomach and she calmed down. Her contractions were strong and Uncle Quincy kept her calm, you know, Dad, like you do. No one can do that but you and Uncle Quincy with cows and horses. You got the touch. And…"

"Take a breath." Jude sat up and watched the excitement on his son's face. Zane had been in bed when Jude had come in last night. He'd stayed longer than he'd expected at Annabel's. He'd wanted her to know the truth and found it easy to talk to her. She understood he wanted to wait until the situation with Paige was over. She didn't want to get involved, either, if his heart was somewhere else. Jude didn't know where his heart was. But then, he did. It was with this little boy whose eyes were sparkling like firecrackers on the Fourth of July.

"It was amazing, Dad, I tell you. Uncle Quincy taped her tail because she was swishing it and then Jenny washed White Dove's udder, teats and vulva with water and soap. And—"

"Vulva?"

"Yeah, it's—"

"I know what it is." He was surprised his son did, but that was Zane. He'd probably read about birthing and knew every detail. Once he learned something, he never forgot it. His memory was uncanny.

"Well, the foal's feet were like this." Zane stuck out his arms as far as he could and placed his head between them. "That's the way she came out, in a white amniotic sac. Jenny said it was a perfect birth and Uncle Quincy agreed. Once the front feet and head and shoulders appeared, it was like swoosh and the rest of it followed into a yucky mess. Jenny's already calling her Little Dove because she's white and black like her mama. It took four attempts before Little Dove could stand on wobbly legs and she's the cutest thing. You should've seen it, Dad. Do you think her legs are long like Bear's 'cause they're related?"

Jude swung his feet to the floor. "Yep, Red Hawk is their father." Zane had seen births before on the ranch, but he was extra excited because he spent a lot of time with Quincy and his paint horses.

"I think I want to be a vet."

Jude stared at his precious son with his hair in his eyes. "How about a scientist or a chemist who discovers a cure for cancer?"

"Cool, Dad. I can do that, too." Zane grinned as he slipped a T-shirt over his head. "After everything was over, Quincy said I better go to the house or Grandma would be worried. He was right. She was sitting up, waiting on me. She said she can't go to sleep unless I'm safely in bed. I'm lucky to have a grandma like that."

"Yes, you are." Jude felt a pang of guilt for staying out so late. He didn't want his mother to stay up and wait for Zane. That was Jude's job. Once in twelve years wasn't bad, though.

"You were out with Ms. Hurley. Did you talk about me?"

"Our favorite topic of conversation."

"Cool, Dad. I'm going to check on Little Dove and then come back and get ready for school so I can find a cure for cancer." His cheeky son had the audacity to wink.

Zane darted out the door and Jude stood and stretched and then made his way to the shower. Today was the day. He would meet Paige for the first time in almost thirteen years. He wondered if she'd changed. Everyone changed in that amount of time. He certainly had. He wasn't that scared teenage boy anymore. Raising a child had toughened him up quickly. He had to stay on his toes to make good choices and cowboy up when things got rough.

That scared boy had become a man ready to take on the world for Zane. He'd never for one minute regretted going back to get his son. But today he would have to explain that decision to Paige. He was prepared now. The scared boy had surfaced for a moment because he was afraid of losing the one thing that mattered the most to him in this world: his son. That bond was rock-solid and Jude knew that better than anyone.

Since he was going to a funeral, Jude put on starched jeans and a white shirt. With his hair combed, his hat in his hand, he headed for the door, only to be stopped by Zane coming through it.

"That was quick." His son had a strange look on his face, one Jude knew well. Something was wrong and he knew not to push or Zane would clam up. "The foal okay?"

"Yeah. She was sucking, so I guess everything's okay."

"Didn't you talk to Uncle Quincy?"

Zane shook his head. "He and Aunt Jenny were curled up in the hay under a blanket asleep, so I didn't wake them."

"You could have. It would have been okay."

With his small shoulders hunched, Zane replied, "I don't know, Dad. It's different now."

"How is it different?"

"Uncle Quincy doesn't have much time for me anymore."

Jude sat on the bed and patted the spot beside him. Quincy had spoiled Zane, just as he'd spoiled Grandpa and everyone else by lavishing his attention on them. He was that type of person.

"Uncle Quincy still loves you and you're still his partner. But life is about changes. Nothing stays the same."

Zane looked up at him. "I think that's a line from a song, Dad."

Jude ruffled Zane's hair. "It's true. Having fun with Uncle Quincy will change, too. You'll want to spend more and more time with your friends and away from the ranch."

Zane's eyes narrowed. "I'm never leaving the ranch."

Jude didn't push it, because they'd had this conversation many times about college and it always upset Zane. "Trust me. You won't always think that way. You'll change. As much as you say you won't, you will. And if you don't, the ranch will always be here. It will always be home."

"And you'll always be here?"

"You bet." There was no place on earth Jude would rather be. Zane got that from him. By Zane's somber expression, Jude knew something else was bothering his son. "What is it, son?"

"Uh… Uncle Quincy and Aunt Jenny were curled up together. Uncle Quincy had his arms around her and they were like one person."

They'd already had the sex talk, so it couldn't be about that. Jude was sweating bullets thinking about how to answer his son.

Zane saved him. "Uncle Quincy really loves Aunt Jenny."

"And she loves him."

"Yeah. That's nice, huh?"

"Yes. You have one more person who loves you."

"Aunt Jenny gives big hugs and she smells good."

"So you see it's a good thing Uncle Quincy found someone."

"Yeah." There was still a slight hesitation in Zane's voice.

"If you want to talk to Uncle Quincy, just go over to his barn and talk to him. He won't disappoint you. I promise."

There was silence for a moment and Jude struggled to find words to soothe his son's bruised heart. Before Jude could find the right words, Zane looked up at him again and asked, "Did you love my mama like Uncle Quincy loves Aunt Jenny?"

Jude's throat closed up and every word he knew dissipated like smoke into thin air. He tried not to show any reaction but knew that wouldn't work. He'd always been honest with Zane, but now he struggled with the truth. He wasn't sure why. It was just difficult to talk about his feelings for Paige, especially with his son.

He swallowed hard. "Yes, I loved your mother more than I can ever tell you. We were inseparable in high school and…"

Zane wrapped his arms around Jude's waist and buried his face against him. "You don't have to talk about her, Dad."

He held his son close. "It's okay. You were conceived in love. That's why you're such a happy kid."

Zane drew back to gaze up at Jude. "I hope she doesn't come back like Eden's mom did. I don't think I would like her. It's just me and you, right, Dad? You and me against the world. We're Rebels and we're rowdy."

"You bet. Now you better get ready for school. Aunt Rachel will be here any minute."

"Okay." Zane stared at Jude. "Why are you all dressed up?"

Jude took a moment. "I'm going to a funeral this morning."

"Oh. I'm sorry someone died."

Jude hugged his son. Zane had this innate softness inside him, making him genuinely considerate and sincere. He was truly sorry someone had died. That was just the way he was. He got that from Paige.

Ruffling his son's hair, Jude said, "We need to get your hair cut again."

Zane pulled back, smiling. He was happy again. "I want to get it cut before the race because I don't want any hair in my eyes when Bear and I zoom past everybody. We're going to win, Dad! Uncle Quincy said so. I filled out the form and put it and my money in an envelope. When are you going to take it in to the paper?"

"I'll take it before I go to the funeral."

"Cool." Zane dashed into his room and came back with the envelope. "It's all there. You just have to give it to Miss Maureen and get my number. I hope it's a nine. Nine is my lucky number. Oh, yeah." Zane danced off to his room.

When had nine become his lucky number? That was news to Jude, but he had a feeling that as Zane grew, a lot of things were going to be news to him. Little boys tended to keep secrets. He knew that for a fact 'cause he'd kept many from his parents. Not biggies, but secrets.

In the kitchen, Falcon, Quincy and Egan were having coffee with their mother.

"So you're waiting till the birth to find out the sex of the baby?" his mother asked Egan.

"Yeah. I just would rather do that and Rachel agreed with me. Although she was very tempted to find out."

Jericho was right. Jude poured a cup and joined them at the table.

"I guess you're going to the funeral." His mother looked at him.

"Yes. I have to see her to test the waters, so to speak. At this point, I'm not sure how much I'll tell her. It depends on how much she wants to hear. I'll play it by ear and hope I make the right decision."

"You will, son," his mother assured him.

Egan twisted his cup. "I stopped by to tell you Rachel's going to the funeral."

Jude started at that news. "Why? I don't remember them being all that close in high school."

"Jude, it's a small school and we all know each other."

"I guess."

"Besides, Angie Hollister is Horseshoe's one-woman welcoming-and-funeral committee. And Rachel's her best friend. They thought it would be nice if someone from the town showed up. And don't worry—Rachel's not going to say anything. She's rather fond of Zane and, trust me, she's going to make sure no one hurts him."

Jude got to his feet. "Is Rachel still picking up Zane for school?" Rachel taught art and she and Egan lived down the road in a house they'd fixed up, so it was ideal for Rachel to give Zane a ride.

"She'll be here any minute," Egan said. "She notified the principal last night she was taking an hour off."

"I better go, then. Zane wants me to drop off the entry form and fee for the race."

"You haven't had breakfast," his mother reminded him.

"I couldn't eat a thing, Mom. I'll catch y'all later."

As he drove into town, Zane's words kept running through his mind. *Did you love my*

mama like Uncle Quincy loves Aunt Jenny?
Oh, yes, he'd loved Paige with all his heart.
They'd been two teenagers who'd desperately
needed someone to love. Someone to listen.
Someone to care.

Paige's mother had been an awful person.
He couldn't believe any mother could be so
vile. She'd told Paige repeatedly that she was
ugly and worthless and would never amount
to anything. Every chance the woman got,
she'd driven home that point to make Paige
feel as low as she could. She'd shredded Paige's
confidence until Paige was a walking case of
nerves. Sometimes she'd break out in hives
just from the stress.

Looking back, he realized there'd been so
many options open to them other than listening to Mrs. Carstairs, but at the time they
hadn't seen them. Jude could've gone to his
mother and she would've been happy to help
them. But talking was not Jude's strong suit.

He almost would have rather died than tell his mother how he'd screwed up. He was to blame for everything that had happened and he fully carried that blame on his shoulders. If he had spoken up, things would've been different. But he hadn't known how Paige would've reacted if he'd asked her to marry him and give up her dream. He couldn't do that, pressure her to stay in a town that held so many bad memories. She deserved to fulfill her dream more than anyone he'd ever known. He'd made sure she did. Whatever had happened in the intervening years, he hoped with all his heart she was happy and had a full life.

He drove toward the Horseshoe cemetery, ready to face his past.

THE APRIL WIND howled through the tall cedars of Horseshoe's country cemetery. Paige shivered and reached for Staci's hand. The ominous sound was a fitting lullaby for a woman who had been troubled most of her life. The noise would carry on into the hereafter.

They didn't shed tears. There were too many teardrops on their souls to pretend any grief now. Sadness, yes. Paige was sure it showed on their solemn faces as they said goodbye to a mother they'd never understood.

Out of the corner of her eye, she saw a silver SUV pull into the cemetery driveway. Angie Wiznowski and Rachel Hollister got out. They were older, but Paige recognized them, girls she had gone to high school with. Rachel was as beautiful as ever with her blond hair and blue eyes. She was pregnant. A pain shot through Paige but she quickly disguised it. Angie had changed the most. She'd always been sweet and nice but she was positively glowing. What were they doing here?

More cars turned into the cemetery. Angie's mom and Angie's sisters and brother had come. The sheriff and his wife arrived, as did Hardy

Hollister, the DA, and Judge Hollister. Mrs. Peabody and the older ladies of the town came. Some of Paige's teachers also came. Some of Staci's and Luke's friends showed up. The people of Horseshoe offered their condolences and Paige was overwhelmed with a nostalgic feeling for a town she'd left behind.

As everyone stood around the grave site, the man from the funeral home read some verses from the Bible and the casket was lowered into the ground. A turbulent life was over.

Angie hugged her. "We're so sorry for your loss."

"Thank you," she managed.

Rachel hugged her, too. "It's so good to see you and you look absolutely wonderful. I guess the California good life agrees with you."

Paige didn't know how to answer. If they only knew. But they never would, because Paige would never open up with all the heartache and pain she'd suffered in the past years.

After everyone had left, Angie and Rachel lingered and they talked about Horseshoe and things that had happened while Paige had been gone. Angie was married to Hardy Hollister, Rachel's brother, which Paige had guessed by the way Hardy had hugged Angie. They had two children. Rachel had married Egan, Jude's older brother. That caught Paige's attention. She'd never known Rachel liked the Rebel boys. She seemed happy, as did Angie. Paige would never have that kind of happiness. She had destroyed her one chance at love.

"We have company," Rachel said as a pickup pulled up behind the SUV.

Angie hugged her one more time. "Come by the bakery before you leave and we can catch up on old times and hear about your amazing career." Angie's family owned the local bakery, a favorite hangout and the busiest place in town.

Paige didn't say anything, because she didn't

plan on taking Angie up on her offer. She wouldn't talk about her life to anyone. She'd opened up last night to Staci and Luke because she had to tell them. She couldn't keep lying and holding everything inside. As family members who had been through hell with her, they understood. But the people of Horseshoe wouldn't, even friends like Angie and Rachel.

They walked away and Paige stared at the man getting out of the truck. Her breath caught and her body trembled as she stared at the boy who was now a man. The boy she'd loved more than anyone in her life.

He walked toward them with long strides. He'd changed, was her first thought. The skinny boy had filled out and his shoulders were wide and muscled. But his beautiful face, carved with the touch of an angel, was the same: dark eyes flanked by incredible eyelashes and lean structured facial bones that bespoke pure masculinity. He'd been a cowboy then and she was delighted to see he was still in boots, a Stetson and snug Wranglers. From out of nowhere a memory flashed through her mind of a lazy afternoon and her unzipping them. She was suddenly warm all over.

Luke met him and they shook hands. Paige couldn't hear what they were saying, but soon Jude walked toward her.

She said the first thing that came into her head. "Hey, Jude." It was the title of an old Beatles song that had been their favorite back then. They'd played it over and over just to sing "Hey, Jude."

He didn't smile, and a foreboding feeling came over her. "I'm sorry about your mom."

"Th-thank y-you." She stumbled over the words like a teenager. "I was going to call before I left town."

"Could we go somewhere and talk?" He looked around at the tombstones and graves nestled among stately cedars. "Someplace be-sides here?"

"Sure. I can use Staci's car. Where would you like to meet?"

"They redid the park that's two blocks from your old house. It's nice and we could meet there."

"Okay. I'll see you in about thirty minutes."

He nodded and strolled back toward his truck.

They were cordial and polite like strangers, but they had been so much more.

"What did he want?" Staci asked.

"Just to talk."

"You don't have to do that if you don't want to," Luke told her. "It might be best to let it go."

"I can't. I have to know if he thinks about our child all the time…like…I do."

"Oh, Paige." She didn't even know she was shaking until Staci put her arms around her.

"I didn't think it would be this hard to see

him." She brushed away an errant tear. "He didn't even smile when I said, 'Hey, Jude.' It was our favorite song."

"Do you still love him?"

She didn't know, but she knew what the nausea was about. Jude. Seeing him again. And having to talk about that time and what they'd done. They had to drag out all the dirty laundry to see if it could be cleansed or if the stains of life's mistakes would haunt her forever.

Chapter Four

Jude parked at the curb of the new Horseshoe Park and made his way to where he saw Paige sitting at a picnic table. The brightly colored swings and slides and the new water park faded from his mind as he focused on the woman waiting for him.

The first thing he'd noticed at the cemetery was that she'd lost a lot of weight. Away from her criticizing mother, she must've stopped the binge junk-eating. She was now slim and her hair was more blond than brown. It suited her. Her face still held that same sweet innocence that had first attracted him to her. But now there was a maturity about her that was just as attractive.

Never Never Land never looked so good.

She got up and ran to him, then wrapped her arms around his waist and hugged him. The scent of lilac soap wafted to him. He froze, which was more the reaction of the teenage boy he used to be. But the man in him recognized all those old feelings that had bound him to her years ago. Maybe some things just never changed.

When he didn't return the hug, she went back to the table and he eased onto the bench across from her, removing his hat. The wind rustled through the tall oaks and he took a moment to gather his thoughts. It was like gathering bits and pieces from his past to guide him. What should he say? What should he do?

"You look good," she said. "You filled out. The teenage boy I used to date doesn't seem to exist anymore."

"He grew up, and so have you. I hardly recognized you at the cemetery. The young girl of long ago has matured into a beautiful woman."

"Thank you." She tilted her head slightly to smile at him and his heart raced like a wild mustang's at the look he remembered well. "You were always good for my ego."

He didn't shift or act nervous. He couldn't do that now. He had to be the man he was supposed to be. For Zane. And for himself.

"I'm sorry about your mom."

She shrugged. "Thanks. She's at peace now."

"So you've forgiven her for all the crappy stuff?"

"It's hard to hold on to all that bitterness. After Staci put her in the mental hospital, we found out her erratic behavior was because of the injuries to her head and spine in the accident that killed my grandparents. Alcohol only made it worse."

"I knew there had to be a reason for the way

she acted." They were getting bogged down in ordinary conversation when he wanted to talk about something else entirely. "How's California?"

"Great. I'm busy, so I don't get to see a lot of it. But I've enjoyed my stay there."

"I'm glad you had the chance to make your dream come true." He really meant that with all his heart. But a small part of him wanted her to love him enough to have stayed and raised their son together.

"Do you still work on the ranch?" she asked quickly, as if she wanted to change the subject.

"Yes. I'll always be a cowboy."

She fiddled with her hands in her lap. "I heard you have a son." Her eyes caught his and all the guilt hit him, blindsiding him.

"Yes." *Our son. The one you gave away.*

She looked off to the tall oaks and the branches swaying in the breeze. "Do...do... you ever think about our child?"

His stomach roiled with a familiar ache. "Every day." He didn't try to avoid the subject, because he knew they'd have to discuss it thoroughly.

"I think about the baby all the time. I can't seem to shake all those guilty feelings and... and I think we made a mistake."

His gut tensed. "Why do you say that? We talked about it a lot and you said you could handle the feelings. You said the fact that our child would have a good home would be enough for you. What made you change your mind?"

She placed a hand over her heart. "I just have this need to know if I have a son or a daughter. We should have asked. We should have held our child. As a young girl, I was arrogantly boastful that I could handle all those emotions and all those feelings. I was wrong. It almost destroyed me."

"What do you mean?"

"I cried all the way to California and I cried for days afterward. I couldn't get over it. But that's in the past." She waved a hand to dismiss it. "I wanted to talk to you because I was hoping you felt the same and would want to know if we had a son or a daughter. Would you be willing to go with me to talk to Mrs. Carstairs? Maybe she would tell us if we both went."

"Paige…"

"I know you have a different life now and I don't want to interfere with that. But I have to know. Do you understand that?"

He didn't understand anything and he certainly hadn't expected this from her at this late date. He hadn't expected any guilty feelings from the woman whose career meant everything to her and who'd been positive she could handle the emotions. He searched for words to tell her the truth but they stuck in his throat like a wad of cotton.

"If both of us went, she might tell us if the

baby was a boy or girl. We're not asking for our child back, just information. I'd really like to know if our child is happy. Don't you want to know these things?"

We have a son and he's with me. I've had him since the day after he was born. Simple words. Painful words. All he had to do was say them and it would ease her mind. He took a deep breath and tried to force the words out. Before he could, his cell buzzed. He reached into his pocket and pulled it out and saw it was Zane's school. He clicked the call on immediately.

"Excuse me," he said to Paige and got to his feet.

"Mr. Rebel, this is Sharon Thompson, Principal Bowers's secretary."

"Is there a problem?"

"We had an incident at school this morning and the principal would like for you to come in as soon as you can."

"Is my son okay?"

"Yes."

"I'll be there in ten minutes."

He shoved his phone back into his pocket and then picked up his hat. "I'm sorry—I have to go. Can we meet later?"

"I'm staying for two weeks. We're going to clean out our old house and put it on the market. You can catch me over there. Here's my cell number."

"Good. I'll see you then." He marched off without a backward glance, worried about his son. What had happened? Zane was never in trouble.

Jude made it to the school in record time. The school was shaped like a horseshoe. The administration office was in the center, with grades one through six on the left and grades seven through twelve on the right. The gym and cafeteria were in the back. The Horseshoe school system had always been in one spot, but the school was bursting at the seams because the town's population was growing. Soon they would have to have portable buildings to house some of the students.

He went through the double doors into the school. The principal's office was straight ahead and he hurried there. The halls were empty and the big clock on the wall said it was only five after ten.

"Jude."

He turned to see Annabel coming toward him in a spring dress and heels. She was beautiful, patient and loving. Everything he wanted in a woman. He wasn't sure why he held back on taking their relationship further.

"Where's Zane?"

She nodded at a door. "He's in there with Rachel. She's taking care of him."

"Taking care of him? What happened?" Fear edged its way up his spine and his nerves tightened.

Annabel touched his arm. "Calm down. Zane is fine."

Her touch had a calming effect. He took a long breath. "What happened?"

"After first class, the kids went to their lockers to get ready for second period. Dudley Mc-Cray was bragging about how fast his horse was and how he was going to win the Founder's Day Horse Race. Zane told him he had a fast horse, too, and he just might win. Dudley got mad and said no egghead Rebel was beating him. He then pushed Zane and Zane fell backward onto the floor, his books going everywhere. The kids rushed to help him, but he got to his feet, saying Dudley was upset because he was afraid Zane was going to beat him. Dudley told him he wasn't afraid of any egghead Rebel. Zane replied that only idiots weren't afraid. That really got Dudley angry and he went after Zane, but the hall monitor was there and several teachers kept him from hitting Zane again."

"Zane's not hurt?"

"No, he was very calm. I have to get back to class. I'll talk to you later." She gave him a smile and walked off down the hall. He watched her for a moment, thinking she could be his future, but he was tied to the past with a boulder around his neck pulling him down. Why he kept holding on, he wasn't quite sure. But the days ahead would provide closure or more heartache.

He opened the classroom door and went inside. Zane was sitting in a class chair and a very pregnant Rachel was stroking his hair as if to soothe him, and his son was eating it up.

"Hey, Dad." Zane jumped to his feet when he saw Jude.

Rachel kissed the top of Zane's head and said, "Your dad's here and I have to get back to class."

"Did they tell you what happened?"

"Yeah. Are you okay?" He looked Zane over to see if he had bruises or scratches on his face or arms.

"Yes. You told me to never fight unless it was necessary and it wasn't. I can hurt Dudley with words. He's an idiot. He thinks he's going to win the race, but he's not. You and Uncle Quincy said I have the fastest horse."

Jude squeezed his son's shoulder. "Son, we believe that Bear is fast, but a lot of things can happen in a race and I want you to be prepared for that."

"Okay, Dad. But Bear can win."

Jude squatted in front of his son. "I will be there supporting you all the way. I want you to do something for me, though."

"What?"

"I want you to stop bragging about Bear at school. At home, that's different. We'll let Bear do all the talking on race day."

Zane winked. "Gotcha, Dad."

Sharon opened the door. "The principal will see you now."

Jude stood. "Are you ready?"

"I've never been to the principal's office before." For the first time a note of anxiety entered Zane's voice.

Jude patted his son's back. "It won't be so bad."

As they walked toward the principal's office, Zane asked, "Did you ever have to go to the principal's office?"

"Yep. Your uncle Phoenix got me into a lot of trouble with his antics." And Paige. They'd been caught kissing in his truck after the bell had rung and had been sent to the principal's office. He wouldn't share that, though.

"Did you get punished?"

"Not as much as we got punished at home. We couldn't go anywhere on Saturday or Sunday. We had to work."

"Are you going to punish me?"

"No, son. The principal will take care of all that."

The meeting was short. Zane was sent back to class and told all talk of the race was off-limits in school. Dudley was sent to a class-room by himself to read alone and think about what he'd done.

Jude sat outside in his truck for a while re-flecting on those days of long ago. He and Paige had been too young to get involved so seriously. But no one could have told them that at the time. Even so, Jude would never regret having Zane. He wasn't going to apologize to Paige for going back to get him, either. That was his decision and he would stand by it to the day he died.

He started the engine. Now he had to tell Zane's mother about her son. It would be one of the hardest things he would ever have to do.

Paige changed out of her suit into jeans, a T-shirt and sneakers. They were cleaning out the house and it was dirty work. Dust and cobwebs were everywhere, emphasizing all the pain and sorrow that had happened within the walls.

"Hey, the refrigerator still works. How about that?" Staci diligently wiped it out with bleach and water. Staci had had the electricity turned on days ago so they could work. They had two weeks and they planned to repaint inside and out to make it attractive to a buyer.

The house was a nice three-bedroom two-bath brick home their mother had bought with the insurance money from her parents' death. Or more to the point, Uncle Harry, Darlene's guardian, had bought it for them. Uncle Harry and Aunt Nora had lived next door and they had been a godsend when they were growing up. Uncle Harry had died when Paige was fifteen. And Nora had followed six months later.

For the first time the three Wheeler children were alone in the world. But Luke had already joined the army and that left just Staci and Paige and their mother.

Uncle Harry's house had been willed to the three children, but Darlene had sold it and made them sign the papers. With the money, she'd bought a new car and a used one for Staci. She'd blown the rest on frivolous stuff. They didn't live that far from the school and after Staci graduated and went to work, Paige walked to school. But after she fell in love with Jude, he always picked her up.

Jude.

He'd gotten her through high school. He'd gotten her through so much of her horrendous life. And then…

"How did your talk go with Jude?" Staci asked, frowning at the pan of dirty water from cleaning the fridge. "We can keep our cold drinks in here while we're working and that's probably it. The owners will probably dump it."

"We didn't get to talk much. He got a call from the school about his son and he left quickly."

"Did he say anything about his son or his wife or girlfriend?"

"No, and I really don't want to know. I just want him to go with me to talk to Mrs. Carstairs."

Staci stopped what she was doing to look at Paige, who was throwing items from the cabinets into a big trash can. "Kiddo, do you think that's the best decision? It's been a long time and it might be best for you, for everyone, to let it go."

"I can't, Staci. I need answers to go on." Paige leaned against the cabinet. "I've made so many bad decisions and I know I can't go back and change that. But to go forward I have to feel good inside about what happened. I don't know if that's ever going to happen, but I know I have to have some answers."

"Did Jude say he would go with you?"

"He didn't say much of anything, but that's Jude. He doesn't talk much. He said he would come by here when he got through at school and I'm going to ask him again."

Staci closed the refrigerator and wiped her hands on her jeans. "I don't mean to hurt you, but how is knowing you had a son or daughter going to help you feel any better? The baby is still gone. I think it's time you face that. That's the only thing that's going to give you closure. Just be grateful you gave the child a life and probably a very good one with a nice family who's spoiling the devil out of it."

"But I'll never know." A sob clogged her throat and she took a moment to get her emotions under control. "It was so important to me to leave Horseshoe and Darlene behind that I couldn't see I was also leaving the most important part of me behind. Looking back, I get so mad at Jude for not speaking up and saying that we couldn't give the baby away. But he never said anything and now..."

"What difference would that have made?"

"What?"

"You were all set to go to Berkeley. What would you have done with the baby?"

"I don't know!" Paige wailed. "I just..."

"Oh, honey." Staci stepped over the junk on the floor and hugged Paige. "You've got to sort all this out and let go or you're never going to have any peace."

Paige wiped away a tear. "I should've talked to you. I should've talked to someone other than the counselor."

"Why didn't you? I know I was working a lot, but I've always been here for you. I never dreamed you were pregnant. You never shared that."

"Darlene... She said I would never amount

to anything. I would wind up pregnant and living off welfare. I just couldn't let that happen. I couldn't..."

"Honey, you need to see a therapist or something. That's the only way you're going to be able to deal with this. Jude can't help you. He's moved on and has a life of his own now. I'll look for someone in Austin. Someone who you can trust and confide in and who has answers that can help you."

"I'm leaving in two weeks. I have to get back to my job. To my life. I'll be fine. It's just hard coming back here and facing the biggest mistake of my life."

Luke came in from the back door, interrupting them. "I have the truck loaded down with junk from the backyard. I'm taking it to the dump. I can take a few more things."

"There are several bags of trash," Staci said. "I'll help you load it."

Paige continued to wipe down the cabinets,

her thoughts tumbling around like clothes in a dryer, round and round. She stopped as one thought became clear. There was no way to make her feel better. No counselor could do it. Jude couldn't do it. It was something Paige had to deal with on her own. Keeping a secret locked up inside for so long hadn't helped her. Her brother and sister were shocked at her actions. Paige was, too. There was a mixed-up young girl somewhere deep inside Paige whom she had to forgive. That was her magic. She had to forgive herself. And she had to let go of her child and let it have the life that she had given it. There was no way to go back.

And she had to stop blaming Jude.

She drew a jagged breath as the truth of that ran through her system. She had to forgive herself. That was her saving grace.

Staci came in. "Luke said when he gets back, he's going to mow the yard and start scraping the trim on the outside of the house. And you and I can start on the inside. But first we have to go into Temple to buy some paint."

"Do you mind if I stay here? I don't want to miss Jude." She wanted to apologize for her crazy actions earlier. There was no way Mrs. Carstairs would give her any information and she now understood that. She wanted her child protected at all costs. That was the only thing she could give it now.

"Paige…"

"I'm okay. We just need to talk. To say good-bye for good and I'll wish him well. We have a connection that will never be broken."

Staci eyed her. "You seem better."

"I've come to my senses. I can't go back." She shrugged. "I guess I was trying to rewrite the past. Wouldn't it be wonderful if we could do that?"

"Mmm." Staci grabbed her purse. "I'll see you later."

After Staci left, Paige started wiping baseboards and windowsills, basically ridding the house of all the dirt collected over the years. The bathrooms were a nightmare, but they were sparkling clean when Paige finished. Suddenly, the sound of a truck hummed from outside.

Jude.

Chapter Five

As he stared at the brick house, the past swelled around Jude once again. He'd lost track of the number of times he'd sat out here in his truck waiting for Paige. Most of the time she would come running out the door with her mother screaming behind her. The woman would be yelling vile things like "You're nothing but a slut sleeping around with that boy" or "If you get pregnant, you're on your own. I'm not taking care of any more brats."

Paige would get in his truck crying and he'd drive somewhere private so he could hold her until she felt better. Their whole relationship had been about making each other feel better. Jude had been dealing with a lot of emotion from his dad's death and being with Paige had eased his turmoil. It had to have been the saddest relationship on record. For once Jude wanted to feel some happiness and not wake up every morning with a giant knot in his stomach. Today he would start that process, because he was tired of feeling guilty and tired of all the stress. He wanted a life—for him and his son.

He got out and walked through the weeds to the front door. The dirty tan trim paint was peeling and he could see a lot of work needed to be done on the house. But homes were always in demand in Horseshoe and they shouldn't have a problem selling the place. Before he could knock, Paige opened the door and he stood completely still as the sight of her blindsided him once again.

Her hair was up in a ponytail, her green eyes

vivid, and she wore jeans and a T-shirt, just like that girl of long ago. Dust lingered on her hair, her face and her clothes, and she'd never looked more beautiful. He grew weak from the sight, for he'd felt sure he was over Paige. They just had to talk about Zane. That was it. Wasn't it?

"Come in," she said, opening the door wider.

He followed her into a bright green kitchen with faded green gingham curtains. He'd been in the house only a couple of times. The wood table and chairs were still in the middle of the kitchen and she sat down, as did he, placing his hat on the table.

"Is everything okay with your son?" she asked as if she knew his son well.

"Yes. Everything's fine." But everything wasn't. He struggled once again with words.

"I'd offer you something to drink, but we don't have anything yet. Staci will probably bring something later."

"Thanks, I'm fine." He looked around the bare room. "Luke and Staci not here?"

"No, Luke's taken a load of trash to the dump ground and Staci's gone into Temple to get paint and supplies."

Privacy. Exactly what they needed.

"Luke has really filled out and Staci looks different, just like you."

"Yeah, we survived." Her mouth turned up at the corners.

"Life was a little crazy back then."

"Yeah." Paige brushed dust from her jeans. "How's your family?"

"Great. Leah came back and now she and Falcon have a year-old son."

Paige's eyes lit up. "That's wonderful. Everyone was so worried about her."

"It's a long story, but Falcon, Leah and the kids are all happy now."

"A happy ending," she murmured with a sad undertone.

"Quincy's married, too," he said to change the subject. "He married Jenny Walker."

She lifted her eyes to his. "Jenny? She dated Paxton, but I don't think he was as serious about her as Jenny was about him."

"She finally figured that out and fell in love with Quincy. And, of course, Egan married Rachel and they're expecting their first child."

"That was a surprise."

"To everyone." Jude relaxed, as he always did when talking to Paige. It was something they did really well.

"And your mom and grandpa?"

"Mom is fine, running the ranch, and Grandpa is Grandpa. Grouchy some days and loving the next. He's getting a little senile and we keep close tabs on him. Elias lives with him and has taken up most of the responsibility."

"Elias?" A bubble of laughter left her throat and he was captivated. "He's the most irresponsible brother, as I remember. Always eager to fight."

"Now, don't bad-mouth Elias. He's changed a lot. He works hard and he plays hard, but he's there if you need someone."

"I think that's a Rebel tradition."

"Yeah." He stared into her warm eyes and couldn't look away. Where was his willpower?

"Where are Paxton and Phoenix?"

"They're on the rodeo circuit, winning and making money and enjoying life."

"That sounds like them. They'll probably never settle down."

"Probably not. They have wanderlust in their blood."

"Unlike you." She held his gaze and he was getting bogged down in an attraction he desperately wanted to deny.

"I'll never leave the ranch. That's just me." For some reason, he felt a need to say that. It wasn't clear in his mind why, but the words were important to him.

"Does everyone live on the ranch?"

"Yep. As I said, Elias lives with Grandpa in Grandpa's house, and Falcon and Leah and their kids live in the old family house. Paxton, Phoenix and Jericho, a friend of Egan's, live in the bunkhouse, Quincy and Jenny are building a new house, and Egan and Rachel live in a house they've renovated."

"Where do you live?"

All the warm feelings disappeared and a cold ball of reality slammed into his stomach. He had the urge to shift nervously, but he'd outgrown that behavior. But the inclination lingered.

"My son and I live with Mom in the big house." The words tasted like dust on his tongue and he hated that reaction. He had nothing to be ashamed of. He had to remain strong.

Her green eyes were puzzled and he could

almost see the questions gathering in her mind. "How about you? Are you in private practice or do you work for a hospital?"

Her head was bent as she stared down at something on her jeans and for a moment he thought she wasn't going to answer. "I was going to lie, but I'm tired of lying and I'm tired of secrets. I'm still in my medical residency. I have about three months before taking the Medical Licensing Exam."

"What? But it's been—"

"I know how long it's been, Jude." She got up and walked to the kitchen window and looked out into the backyard. "As I told you earlier, I cried all the way to California and I cried for days after. Actually, I couldn't stop crying for two months. I couldn't go to class. I couldn't eat. I couldn't do anything but sink into a well of depression."

Jude hadn't been expecting this and it took a few seconds for him to understand what she was saying. As per his old nature, he didn't say anything, because he had a feeling she had a lot more to get off her chest.

"I lost my scholarship and got kicked out of the dorm. I had nowhere to go and—"

"Why didn't you come home?" The words burst out, as he could no longer stay quiet.

"To what? To my mother saying she was right? The criticism and the shame was just something else I couldn't handle."

He clamped his jaw tight to keep the words in. He had to give her time to say everything she needed to.

"I had to go to a homeless shelter and they had toys there for children. I latched on to a teddy bear with a plaid ribbon around its neck. I clung to it day and night and I prayed it was my child. I think I had a nervous breakdown, but I was never diagnosed. I just lay in bed holding that teddy bear. Holding on to it was the only thing that kept me anchored."

"Paige…"

"The counselor came in two to three times a week to talk to people to try to inspire them to get jobs and to take control of their lives. She took an interest in me and I will forever be grateful for that. She listened to all my pain and she cried with me and she gave me hope. I told her my dreams and she said I could still have my dreams, but I told her my dream was not worth anything without my baby." Her voice wavered on the last word and Jude's stomach constricted so tight he couldn't breathe.

He cleared his throat. "You had ten days to change your mind. Did you forget that?"

She turned from the window and wiped away tears. "By the time I could tell her everything, ten days were long past and I had to accept that what I'd done was final, just like it was the day I left."

"You could have called me. You could—"

"Jude, please, let me finish."

He leaned back in the chair, his body tense and his heart desperately close to exploding with so much anger at what had happened to two naive teenagers.

"About eight months later, I showed her the contract that I had still stuffed into my suitcase and she said she didn't know Texas law all that well but she was positive that the adoption for my child was complete. It took about a month for me to accept that."

Jude curled his hands into fists and he wanted to pound on the table until something made sense. All it would've taken was a phone call and Paige could have seen her baby son and rectified a horrible mistake. How was he going to tell her now? The words rushed to his throat and he yearned to let them spill out, but he listened as she continued.

"Her name was Althea Wexton and she got me a job in a hospital answering phones and she encouraged me to get my life back on track. She helped me to file an appeal to get my scholarship reinstated. It took a while, but I finally got some of it back. She also found me a home with an older friend of hers who rents rooms. Ms. Whitman was a sweetheart. She let me live there until I started making some money and was able to pay my rent. Between my job and going to school, I was busy, but at night I still held that teddy bear."

She took a breath and it was an effort for Jude to remain quiet. For a man who didn't speak much, he wanted to start shouting, but he waited as patiently as he could.

"I went to school during the day and worked at night. I had very little sleep, but I didn't need much. Thea and Ms. Whitman were my cheerleaders. There truly are nice people in this world and I couldn't have gotten through the past twelve years without them. Perfect strangers and they feel like my family. I have three job offers when I finish my residency and my dream is finally going to come true. But it feels like a hollow victory."

"Did you call Staci during that time? Did you tell her about the baby?"

"No. I couldn't tell anyone."

"Why didn't you just come home? I would've sent plane tickets or come and got you. All you had to do was call."

She brushed a stray curl behind her ear. "Home to what? To listen to my mother say 'I told you so.' Home to the shame and humiliation. There was nothing for me here."

"Not even me?"

Their eyes collided in a wave of remembered love, of all the good times and all of the regrets.

"I didn't think there was any way for us to go back and be those two young people so much in love. We'd done the unforgivable and would always blame each other." She swiped a tear from her cheek. "I got a little emotional this morning asking about our baby. I realize we can't go searching for answers. That's out of the question. It's just coming back to Horse-shoe has made me regret so many things."

"I'll never regret loving you."

Her eyes filled with more tears. "How did we make such a bad decision?"

"We were too young to see other options, and there were other options."

"Like what?"

"We could have gotten married and raised the baby like Falcon and Leah did, but I knew your heart was set on leaving and I never asked. That was my fault. I should've been more assertive and taken more responsibility for the child you carried."

"Oh, Jude, don't say any more." She turned back toward the window. "This is just too hard. Could you please leave?"

"Do you still sleep with the teddy bear?"

She swung around, confusion on her face. "Why?"

"I'm just curious."

"I could lie, but what's the use? Yes, the teddy bear is at Staci's apartment. I take it everywhere I go. It's my security blanket. I'm a medical professional and I cling to a teddy bear just to get me through the night."

Jude got to his feet, feeling stronger than he had in a very long time. "I know where our child is."

Paige's eyes opened wide and she took a step backward and reached for the counter for support. "How...how do you know that? Did Mrs. Carstairs tell you? Is the baby here in Texas? Oh!" She covered her mouth with shaky hands.

He took a couple steps toward her. "On the drive back to the ranch I kept thinking about my dad and what he told us about taking responsibility if we ever got a girl in trouble. How we should stand up and do the right thing and be a Rebel. A Rebel takes care of his own. I just felt I had let my father down and I had let my child down. I couldn't live with that. I went home and I told my mother what we'd done."

"You told your mother?"

He swallowed hard. "Yes, and it will forever be imprinted upon my brain. Something I thought would be extremely difficult was rather easy. She called her brother, Gabe, a lawyer, and we went back to the hospital."

"What?"

Speaking became difficult and he had to take several deep breaths. "I told the administrator of the hospital I wanted my baby. I was so afraid the adoptive parents had already left with it, but the baby had a cough and the doctor was checking it out."

"What?" Paige's face turned a pasty white.

"Since it was a private adoption, the administrator called the adoptive parents' attorney. I stuck to my guns. I wanted my kid. Gabe looked at the contract and it was my option to change my mind and I did. The attorney was ready to fight, saying I needed your consent to take the baby, but everything fell into place once we learned who the adoptive parents were."

"Who?"

"Mrs. Carstairs and her husband."

"What? No!" What little color was left on Paige's face drained away.

"She wanted your baby. That's why she gave you information that fed on your weaknesses and your fears. Once Gabe learned this, he threatened to file charges against her and her husband and to inform the Horseshoe school board of her actions concerning young girls in the school. They folded quickly. They brought the baby out and my mom and I took it home. Our baby has been with me ever since the day after the birth."

Chapter Six

"What?"

"Our child is with me, safe, loved and cared for. You don't have to wonder anymore."

The room swayed with an inky darkness and Paige reached out to grab the counter to keep from crumpling to the floor. Her body trembled.

She grappled with what Jude was saying and was vaguely aware that he had taken her shoulders and guided her to a chair.

"You…you went back. You went back. You went back." She couldn't stop saying the words, over and over, as if by doing so, they would be completely true and she could hold her child in her arms. She could see its face. She could…

Jude gently shook her. "Paige, stop it!"

She was on the brink of sinking into a hole so deep she could never find her way out. But then she heard his voice. The voice that had always soothed and comforted her. She looked into his concerned eyes. "You have our child?"

He pulled a chair closer and sat facing her, within touching distance. "Yes."

So many questions rumbled around in her head like thunder, piercing and jarring, but one thing she had to know was at the forefront of her mind. "Your son is our…"

"Yes. His name is Zane."

"Zane." She said the word lovingly, rolling it around on her tongue, testing it, loving it. It was a strong name. A Rebel name. *Her* son. She began to tremble again and Jude reached out and clasped her hands.

"He's a bright, funny and happy kid. He's

easygoing and it takes a lot to get him down. He gets frustrated with school because his IQ is the highest ever recorded in the school system, right above his mother's."

Tears slipped from her eyes and she didn't bother to brush them away. They were happy tears. Tears that warmed all the emotions churning through her like waves of glory.

"He loves horses, outer space, technology. He created the ranch's website and keeps it up-to-date. He has all kinds of videos on there and things that go over everyone else's heads. Once he learns something, he's learned it forever. His memory is phenomenal and sometimes it's frightening, the knowledge that he picks up. But inside, he's still a little boy."

"How…how did you manage with a baby?"

"It wasn't easy, but I figured if Falcon could do it, so could I. Of course, I couldn't have done it without my mother's help. She showed me how to change diapers, how to make formula, how to soothe him when he cried. After I got the hang of it, everything else became natural. Luckily, he didn't cry like Eden had. He was a happy baby and started sleeping through the night when he was two months old. I had his crib in my room and sometimes at night I'd touch him just to make sure he was still there and to make sure he was breathing."

"Oh." Without her even realizing it, a moan escaped her throat. She closed her eyes tight and then opened them quickly to see if she was dreaming. She had to be. This couldn't be true. Jude had their son. A son. She had a son.

"When he was a baby, Mom kept him in the office while I worked. We took turns working and looking after Zane. He was about four months old when I bought one of those carriers that strapped around my body and I started taking him with me on the ranch. I changed diapers under shade trees and he took naps on a blanket while we ate lunch. If he grew fussy or something, Grandpa would entertain him. He's the only person in the family who loves Grandpa's stories. He grew up on the rhythm of a horse. I guess that's why he loves horses so much."

"That must have been difficult, though."

"Yes, but my family helped and that's what made it easier. If it was really hot or really cold, one of us would stay behind with Zane at the house or the office. Quincy was a big help, too. He's Zane's second father and Zane confides a lot of stuff to Quincy that he won't tell me. I'm glad my brother is there for him."

"Sounds like he didn't even need a mother."

"But he missed having one."

Through all the wonderful things Jude was saying, one thing kept piercing her happiness. She drew a quivery breath. "What have you told him about his mother?"

Jude pulled back and she missed the warmth of his hands on hers. She desperately needed it and wanted to snatch his hands back, but she remained still.

"The truth."

"The truth?" The trembling became intense and she struggled to catch her breath. "You told him we gave him away?"

"Yes."

"And that you went back to get him?"

"Yes."

"So…so he knows…he knows I gave him away." Each word struck her heart like a hammer and she fought to control her emotions, but she was losing the battle.

"He was about five when he started asking about his mother. He almost thought it was normal since Eden didn't have a mother, either, but he noticed kids in school had mothers, so he wanted to know where his was. I told him that you went away to school to become a doctor and I raised him."

"That's all you told him?"

"Until he was about nine. Then he wanted to know more and I told him the truth because I didn't want him to grow up and learn that I had lied to him. I was always honest and tried to answer his questions honestly."

She sank her teeth into her lower lip to keep from crying out. "He knows. He knows his mother gave him away. He knows..." Hard sobs shook her body. Uncontrollable sobs. After a moment, she gave up and just cried for everything that she had lost. Everything that she could never get back. Her son. Those precious years that she'd been holding a teddy bear, she should have been holding her son. It wasn't Mrs. Carstairs's fault. It was Paige's for being so gullible. No one was to blame but herself. Yet a part of her wanted to blame Jude. A part of her needed to blame Jude.

"Paige, come on. Stop this."

She lifted her head, choking back sobs. "How could you do that to me? How could you tell our son I gave him away? He'll never forgive me and I'll never forgive myself. How could you do that?"

"Paige..."

She jumped up and ran to the bathroom and slammed the door. She had to get away to sort out all the tumultuous emotions chugging through her. Outside the door she heard Staci's voice and knew she was back. Then she heard Luke's and Jude's and Jude was telling them about Zane. Her son.

Sitting on the edge of the bathtub, she cried as if there were no tomorrow. And for her, there wasn't. At least not one where she could live with herself and the mistakes that she'd made. She'd heard it said that life was about making mistakes and learning from them and moving on, but how would she get from point A to point B without having her heart ripped out once again?

Totally spent, she got up and rinsed her face

with cool water. There were no towels, so she pulled up the bottom of her T-shirt and wiped her face. As she did, she took in the drab yellow bathroom that had once been bright yellow. The Southwestern yellow-and-orange-colored tile was atrocious and the years hadn't improved it.

When Paige was pregnant, she would sit in the bathtub and read stories to her baby. She'd had books in her backpack, and no one, not even Jude, had ever known that she read to their son every day. That should have given her a clue about her unstable emotions. Instead she'd told the baby how much she loved it and how she was going to give it a better life than she'd had. What a crock! How could a smart girl have been so dumb?

Taking a long steadying breath, she knew she had to face her past and do something she hadn't been able to do before. She had to face her son.

There was a tap at the door and she considered ignoring it, but that was no way to start the next phase of her life. She unlocked it and Jude came in. His handsome face was lined with worry, much as it had been when she'd told him she was pregnant.

"Are you okay?"

She pushed her hands up her face and drew a cool breath. "No. I'm never going to be okay."

"Paige…"

She stuck out her hand. "I don't want to hear any more. I want to meet my son."

"That's going to take time."

She narrowed her eyes. "What do you mean?"

"I have to prepare Zane and I need time for that."

That sounded reasonable. "Okay. Tomorrow will be fine."

Jude shook his head. "No. Zane is entered in a horse race on Saturday and I'm not going to tell him until after that. This race is important to him and if I tell him now, I don't know what he'll do or say. This is my call and you have to accept it."

"So you're only honest when it suits you."

His tanned skin paled. "As I said, this is my call. I'm doing what's best for my kid."

"He's my kid, too."

"I have full custody of Zane. You signed away your parental rights."

The statement was a blow to her chest. "How dare you say that to me."

The strong, stern lines of his face didn't flinch. "I'll let you know when I tell him. It's his decision whether to see you or not."

"How can you do this?"

"I'm doing what's best for my kid, as I have for the past twelve years. I put my life on hold for him and I'd do it over again in a heartbeat. That boy is my life and I will protect him with every breath I have. I'm not saying this to hurt you, only to protect Zane. This is going to be a blow and he needs time to adjust."

"I would never hurt him."

"Just seeing you is going to hurt him."

"So, what, Jude? You want me to go away?"

"I don't know." He swiped a hand through his hair in frustration. "You say you have two weeks before you have to go back to California. I'm just trying to figure out how Zane fits into your schedule."

She leaned back against the sink as reality intruded upon the wonderful news of her son. Once again she was faced with a monumental choice, but this time she was more mature and more able to handle it. This time she would not leave her son and Jude was not going to lay any kind of a guilt trip on her. Even though she might have deserved one.

She pushed away from the sink. "I'm not leaving until I see my son. Not until I can talk to him and beg his forgiveness. And not until

I have some sort of peace of mind that he is happy. That's what's most important to me."

Jude sighed, as if he'd reached the end of his patience. "Zane is focused on the race right now. That's all he thinks about and it's all he talks about. If I tell him now, it will shatter all his plans and I'm not doing that to him. After Saturday, I will tell him you want to see him and, as I said, it's his decision, not yours."

She looked into his dark eyes, the ones that used to be warm and encouraging and loving. Today they were not. They were cold and unforgiving and layered with something she'd never seen in them before. Anger.

"You blame me, don't you?"

"We can't go back and—"

"How many times did I ask you what we should do? What was your response, Jude? Every time?"

He looked down at his boots.

"You never said a word, Jude. You never said

we had options or anything else. *You never said a word.*"

His gaze crashed into hers. "You had your whole life planned, and how was I supposed to shatter that? You wouldn't have listened to anything I had to say anyway. You listened to that stupid counselor more than you ever listened to me. So, yes, maybe I am laying some of the blame at your feet, but I also know a lot of it was my fault, too. I'm quiet by nature, but believe me, I've learned to speak up and I've learned to protect my son and I will do just that now."

"You…you…you…" She made a dive for him, and with her fists, she pummeled his chest, over and over. "How could you? How could you? I hate you. I hate you!"

He stood there taking the blows, not saying a word, and that made her even angrier.

Staci squeezed past Jude into the small bathroom and grabbed Paige's arms and pulled her away. "Stop it!" She looked at Jude. "You better go. This is getting out of control."

Jude walked out and she heard the front door slam. Staci gathered her into her arms. "Come on, kiddo. You're stronger than this."

"He won't…he won't…" she blubbered.

Staci took Paige's arm and led her to the kitchen and pushed her into a chair. "Take a deep breath." Staci rummaged in a bag on the table and pulled out bottled water. "Drink this."

Paige placed her shaky hands around the bottle and took a big gulp. It was cold, cooling the heated emotions inside her. She was so angry. That was so unlike her. After living for months in a homeless shelter, she'd vowed she would never lose control again. She'd just broken that vow.

Luke hovered near the door, looking at her as if she'd grown another head. Staci had the same expression on her face. What had she done?

Staci pulled a chair close to Paige. "Are you okay?"

Paige gripped the bottle and shook her head. "No."

"Just give Jude some time. This has been a shock to everyone, but you know where your child is now. He's with his father. That's good news."

"But Jude is never going to let me see him."

"Sure he will, but you have to decide what you're going to do. You have to go back to California to finish your residency. It's just like before."

Paige ran her thumb down the cold bottle and thought her life was like a never-ending circle of decisions. Bad decisions. Decisions that hurt. This was the ultimate one and she had already made it and she didn't understand why everyone kept pointing it out. Her son came first, this time. All the anger in her eased at the thought. Jude would not keep her away from Zane. Nothing would.

"His name is Zane," she said for some reason, maybe just to hear it.

"I know, kiddo."

"He's going to hate me." She had to say that, too. Maybe to hear someone else say it wasn't so. She got the answer she wanted.

"No. Kids forgive easily. Just stay positive."

"I just want to see his face. Touch him. Just to see that he's real."

Staci reached over and hugged her. "You will. You just have to be patient."

Something Jude had said triggered a thought. "Where's my phone?"

Staci pointed to the counter and Paige got up and brought it back to the table, touching the keypad on the screen.

"What are you doing?"

"Jude said Zane does the website for the ranch. I'm hoping there might be a picture of him on there. Here it is. Rebel Ranch. Hereford cattle." There were pictures of red cattle with white faces. Heifers for sale. Bulls for sale. Hay for sale. A link reading Rebel Family caught her eye and she clicked it. A picture of all the brothers with Miss Kate and Grandpa Abe in the center came up. No kids. Her heart sank. But then she saw another tab. Family Photos. Grandchildren. She clicked it and her heart almost pounded out of her chest when she saw Eden, a very grown-up Eden, sitting in a comfy chair holding a baby, and a boy was sitting on the chair's arm. Paige tapped the photo until she'd zoomed in on the boy in jeans, boots and a white shirt. He was smiling. Happy. He favored Jude. Her son.

She swallowed the lump in her throat and couldn't take her eyes from the screen. She'd wondered so many times what her child would look like and the photo eclipsed every thought, every picture, in her head. He was perfect. Just like his father.

She tapped, edited, clipped and refocused.

"What are you doing?" Staci asked.

"Making it my screen saver. I want to go into Temple to get some copies made." She got to her feet and headed for the door. Luke caught her before she could open it.

"Sis, take a moment and think about this. Just take a deep breath. You're turning back into that scared, frightened young girl and I know you're not her. You're stronger now. Act like it. You don't need copies of pictures. You need to get your second wind and regroup and wait for Jude. He will not let you down."

A tear leaked from her eye again and another followed. She held on to Luke as the walls that she had built around her heart began to crumble. "I'm falling apart, Luke. Please hold me. Don't let that happen."

Staci ran and wrapped her arms around them. "We're here for you."

"Don't let go!" she cried, and the Wheeler kids stood strong against the waves of despair that rolled over Paige. She had something that she'd never had before. She had strength. She had family. Nothing was going to break her again.

She would wait forever to hold her son. And she would wait for his father, too. Before her healing could even begin, Jude had to forgive her.

And she had to forgive herself.

Chapter Seven

As Jude drove over the cattle guard, rain pelted his truck. He'd been so engrossed in his thoughts that he hadn't even noticed the dark clouds rolling in. By the time he reached the house, the storm vented its full fury with sheets of rain punctuated by lightning and ear-splitting thunder.

He jumped out of his truck and ran into the house. In the utility room, he removed his hat, shook water from it and laid it on the counter to dry. Opening cabinet doors, he found a towel and wiped his face and dabbed at his wet shirt. Since it was raining, his brothers would be in soon. They couldn't work in the rain, so there was no need for him to saddle up and join them. Glancing at the wrought-iron clock on the wall, he saw it was after two. It had been a stressful morning and the time had flown.

He walked through the house to the den, not bothering to turn on a light. He didn't need one. He was still dealing with all the turmoil inside him. Sinking onto the sofa, he took a deep breath, hardly believing that he'd lost his temper with Paige. He'd said things he regretted, but he was fighting for his son. So many emotions warred inside him and he was desperately trying to make sense of it all.

The back door opened. Boots stomped. It wasn't his mother, so it had to be one of his brothers. Phoenix came into the room, dry as could be. Evidently, he'd had his slicker with him.

"Is the electricity off?" Phoenix asked, sliding into a leather chair across from Jude.

"No. I just don't need a light. Is everybody quitting for the day?"

"I'm sure with all this rain, but I had to go with the feed-store fertilizer truck to show the guy where to fertilize the coastal hay in the far west pasture. It's not doing as well as the other fields and Falcon thought it needed a boost. We got it on the ground before the rain. Now as long as it doesn't wash away..."

Jude stared down at his hands, seeing Paige's face, her tears, and his stomach cramped.

"Elias said he's going to kick my ass because I get all the easy jobs. He says I'm Mom's favorite. But, you know, I might just kick his ass for saying that."

"Have you seen Elias's muscles lately?"

"Yeah, how is that possible? He never works out and after work he spends all his time down at Rowdy's. You can't get those kinds of muscles lifting a beer can."

"He does the work of two men. Have you seen him drive a nail into a post?"

"Bam." Phoenix drove a fist into his palm. "One whack and it's done. Takes me two to three tries before the nail goes in."

"Me, too." A small tug at the corners of his mouth, and he found that odd since mirth was the last emotion in his body.

"Hey, hey, look at that." Phoenix pointed. "I made you smile."

The back door opened again and his brothers filed into the living room, followed by Grandpa. Jude didn't want to deal with all of them right now and he had the urge to run as far away as he could. From himself. From all the heartache that was to come.

His brothers sat on the large leather sectional sofa and Grandpa made Phoenix get up so he could take the comfortable chair.

"It went that bad, huh?" Quincy was the first to speak.

Jude stared down at his clasped hands between his knees. "I lost my temper."

"Come on, Jude. You never lose your temper."

"I did this morning with Paige. I said things I regret, but I had to say them."

"What happened?"

His throat felt as if he'd swallowed a pinecone. "I told her about Zane and she wants to meet him."

"And you don't want her to?"

Jude unclenched his hands and told his brothers what Paige had told him. "She's had it rough and I didn't want to hurt her, but Zane comes first with me. He's so excited about the race and if I tell him now, it's going to take all the excitement away. I don't want to hurt him, either."

"That's a tough decision," Falcon said. "It took Eden a long time to warm up to Leah, but once the ice was broken, it's been a love-fest ever since."

"This is different, though. She has three months left on her residency and she goes back to California in two weeks. What kind of relationship can they build in two weeks?"

"You know," Falcon continued, "it took me a long time to forgive Leah and I sense you're feeling similar emotions. I never could understand why she couldn't come home until I got to know what her life was like in Houston without me and Eden."

Jude jumped to his feet as Falcon pointed out the reason for his anger. "All she had to do was call and I would have flown out to get her or sent money for her to come home. All she had to do was pick up the damn phone, but instead she spent months in a homeless shelter, depressed and lonely. All it would've taken was a phone call. Man, that just gets me."

"Get a grip, boy," Grandpa said. "I always

preached to you boys about finding wives, but all this drama is a little hard on my heart. You just make it plain to her that Zane stays here."

"You've always been honest with Zane," Egan spoke up. "If he finds out from someone else in Horseshoe that his mother is here, he's going to wonder why you didn't tell him first."

"He's never asked her name, so he doesn't know it."

"Don't kid yourself, Jude," Egan told him. "Zane's birth certificate is on file at the courthouse, digital now, and with Zane's computer skills, I'll bet every penny I have he's already looked it up. He hasn't asked, because he already knows."

Jude ran a hand through his hair. "Oh, man, I hadn't thought of that."

"Every kid is curious about their parents, and in my humble opinion, I think every kid has a right to meet them at least once in their lifetime."

Everyone stared at Elias. It wasn't like him to offer advice.

"What?" Elias lifted an eyebrow. "I have opinions and some of them are pretty damn good."

Paxton slapped him on the back. "And you're stone-cold sober?"

"Thanks, everybody," Jude said. "But I have to make this decision on my own and it's not easy."

Falcon got to his feet. "We're all here if you need anything, but it's your decision. None of us are going to interfere with that." He turned toward the door. "Now, it would be nice if we got all the tractors and trucks and trailers greased and oiled while the weather is bad."

Elias grabbed Phoenix around the neck. "I know someone who's going to get a little axle grease on his hands and Mama's not here to protect him."

"Come on, Elias. We all know you can pulverize me, but why go to all that trouble. I'm really a nice guy and I fetch really well."

"Good, you can fetch me a beer while we're changing the oil in the trucks and tractors."

His brothers trooped out of the room, but Quincy and Grandpa lingered. "What time does Zane get home from school?" Quincy asked.

"Rachel's bringing him home about four. I got called to the school this morning because there was an incident with Dudley McCray. They got into a thing over the race and Dudley ended up knocking Zane down."

"Did he get hurt?"

"No. Didn't even hurt his pride. He's so hyped up on this race I'm not even sure he's going to hear me if I talk about his mother."

Quincy eyed him. "You don't want to tell him, do you?"

Jude heaved a sigh. "It's not that, but once I tell him, our lives will change. Everything will change. All the joy and happiness that's in his eyes right now will be gone. He won't be a little boy anymore. He'll be a twelve-year-old dealing with some serious issues. I want to protect him from that, but I know I can't. This is what life is about. And it's tearing me apart that Zane is going to feel the pain of Paige's and my decision of long ago."

"But he'll also feel the joy of his dad doing the right thing," Grandpa pointed out.

"Thanks, Grandpa."

Grandpa patted Jude's back. "You've always been a good kid, just like Zane, but don't you let that woman get her claws into him. That's my last word."

Quincy took Grandpa's arm. "Let's let Jude figure this out for himself." As they walked toward the kitchen, Quincy glanced back with a worried look in his eyes. No one was a better brother than Quincy. But now Jude had to step away from the support of his family and determine what to do based on what was right for his son. In the process, he would lose a piece of his heart. But he was a man now and he would handle it better than he had before Zane was born. Because along the way, he'd learned to speak up. And tonight he would say things he'd thought he never would. That was what fathers did.

THAT NIGHT AFTER supper Zane talked and talked about Bear and the race and Dudley McCray. Jude's mom listened with avid interest, but Jude was thinking ahead to when he and Zane were alone.

"You have homework?" Jude asked his son.

"Nah, Dad. I just had to read a book and

I already read it. We'll discuss it in class to-morrow."

"Finish putting dishes in the dishwasher and then go up and take a shower. I want to talk to you for a minute."

Zane's shoulders slumped. "Aw, Dad, I'm okay. We don't have to talk about Dudley any-more. It's over. He didn't hurt me or anything. He just thinks he's a big deal. That's all. I want to ride Bear one more time before bed."

"No. It's dark and you've already ridden Bear for the day."

"Uh-oh, Grandma. I think a blue norther just blew in."

"Go upstairs, Zane."

"Okay, Dad. I'm gone." He darted out of the room.

His mother gave him a dark look. "You're not hiding your feelings very well."

Jude carried his plate to the sink. "I know. I'm nervous and finding this difficult."

"Just calm down and everything will go fine."

"I just hate to shatter his world, but I have to tell him before someone else does."

His mother leaned against the counter, wiping her hands on a dish towel. "I've always known she'd regret her decision, but I never guessed she'd regret it as soon as she got to California. To give a baby away is a traumatic thing and I can sympathize with her feelings because I know Darlene Wheeler was a terrible mother. She inflicted so much mental pain on Paige and that's unforgivable. But it's time for all the hurting to stop, son, and for you and Paige to be as honest as possible with Zane. That's the only way you're going to salvage anything from this. And the only way any of you can go forward."

"I know, Mom. I'm going up to talk to him now." Jude took his time going up the stairs, rehearsing words in his head. But none of them were right. Somehow he had to find a way to tell his son about his mother.

He went through his bedroom and bath into Zane's room. His son sat in the middle of his bed in his underwear and a T-shirt, clicking away on his laptop.

"Want to play a game?" Zane asked.

"Did you take a shower?"

"Yeah, Dad. I'm fast." Jude remembered those days when Zane was little and his bath took about one minute. His face would still be dirty and his fingernails filthy. Jude would have to make him take another bath and scrub clean. Zane hated taking the time. He wanted to be active, doing something else.

"Do I need to look behind your ears?"

"Come on, Dad. I've outgrown that." Zane's eyes went back to the laptop. "Let's play a game."

"No, I need to talk to you first."

"Ah, Dad. I'm okay. Dudley's just a lot of hot air. You don't have to worry about me."

Jude sat on the bed, facing his son. "It's not about Dudley or the McCrays. This is something else."

"Oh." Zane's eyes were big and round, and Jude could almost see the thoughts running through his head. "Does it have something to do with the funeral you went to this morning?"

"Yes." His son had just made it a little easier.

"Do I know this person?"

"No."

"But it made you sad?"

Jude took a moment, not wanting to be cruel. "I hadn't seen this person in a long time so, no, it didn't make me sad."

"Who was it?"

The room became so quiet Jude could hear himself breathing. He swallowed and forced the words out. "Your grandmother."

"Nah. My grandma's downstairs, probably

getting ready to watch television. You…" Zane stopped as he figured it out quickly. "You mean my mother's mother?"

"Yes."

"Was *she* there?"

"Yes, your mother was there."

The light in Zane's eyes went out almost as if he'd flipped a switch. "Did you talk to her?"

"Yes. She's going to be here about two weeks and she would like to meet you."

"No!" Zane threw the laptop on the bed, jumped up and ran into the bathroom. Jude heard him lock the door.

He took a long breath and went to the bathroom door. "Zane, open the door. We need to talk."

Silence. Complete unnerving silence.

"Zane, I'm not going to make you do anything you don't want to. Open the door."

Jude ran out the bedroom door, into his bedroom and to the bathroom. It was empty. Zane was gone. He rushed downstairs. His mother was flipping through the channels on the television.

"Did Zane come through here?"

His mother frowned. "No. I haven't seen him. Why?"

"I told him his mother was in town and wanted to see him and he ran. He has to be somewhere in the house."

"I'll help you look."

He and his mother searched every room and closet but Zane was nowhere to be found. Fear lay in Jude's belly like sour milk and he fought the sick feeling. He had to find his son.

"I'm going to check the barns. Stay here just in case he comes out when I leave. He might talk to you."

"I will. Don't worry, son. He has to be here somewhere."

Jude thought the same thing as he hurried to the big barn, but Zane wasn't there. Then he dashed over to Quincy's barn. Quincy and Jenny were coming out of the small trailer they lived in while they were working on the new house. Quincy had on shorts and a T-shirt and Jenny wore only a T-shirt. Her brown hair was tousled, as was Quincy's. It was clear they were in their own private world.

"Sorry to bother you, but have you seen Zane?"

"No," Quincy replied. "He went to the house a long time ago. What happened?"

"I told him his mother was in town and he ran away. I can't find him. I'm going to check your barn."

"Go ahead."

"We'll help," Jenny offered.

They begin searching the horse stalls and Jude's heart stopped as he saw a small figure crouched in a corner of Bear's stall. He walked to where Quincy was searching.

"I've found him. He's in Bear's stall. Could you give me some time with him, please?"

"Do you want me to—?"

"No," Jude stopped him. "I have to talk to him and no one else."

"Sure. We'll be in the trailer if you need anything."

"Thanks. Would you call Mom and let her know I found him?"

Quincy nodded and they left the barn. Jude took a long breath and went back to the stall. Quietly, he opened the half door and went inside. Bear neighed and moved around in agitation. Jude stroked his face to calm him and then made his way to the corner where his son sat crouched, almost as if he wanted to disappear.

He eased to the hay beside him, not saying a word. Zane sat with his knees drawn up, his forehead resting on his knees, and his hands were folded on the top of his head, blocking his ears as if he didn't want to hear anything anyone had to say. Jude searched for words to ease his son's pain. He went with the truth, as he always did.

"I love you and I will never force you to do anything you don't want to. I hope you understand that."

Silence followed. Zane didn't even move, huddled in the corner in nothing but his underwear and T-shirt. The sight of his young son hurting tore at Jude's heart.

"When you turn eighteen, people say you're an adult, but that's not quite true. You're somewhere between a kid and an adult and it's a precarious place to be because nothing in life makes any sense. You try to make good decisions and hope for the best. Your mother and I were still kids who were faced with grown-up decisions. I've told you some of what happened back then, but now I'm going to tell you the whole truth. It's not pretty and your mother and I are both to blame for what happened."

The barn was dark now and the only light Quincy had on provided little illumination. That was just as well. What Jude had to say he'd rather say in the dark so he could get it all out without breaking down.

Zane kept sitting in the same position, giving the impression that he was trying to pretend Jude wasn't there.

"Your mother and I had a special relationship. I had just lost my dad and she had a mother who was verbally abusive. She would tell her that she was ugly and she would never amount to anything. Every day she heaped criticism after criticism upon her. Some days she'd break out in a rash and scratch until she drew blood. It was very stressful for me to watch and I vowed I would help her any way I could to get out of that house. Your mother worked very hard in school and she got the grades she needed to get a good scholarship for premed. She was happy and I was happy for her. She would get out of Horseshoe and have a life away from a woman who denigrated her every day of her life."

Bear neighed again as if he were annoyed that someone was in his stall. Jude ignored him as he tried to tell Zane what had happened back then.

"Then your mother found out she was pregnant and we didn't know what to do. I wanted her to have her dream and to get away from her mother. I wanted her to have a better life. One of the counselors in school spoke to her about adoption and I never said a word. When she asked me time and time again about what to do, I never spoke up. That was my fault. I should've said I didn't want to give away my kid. But I was caught between my feelings for her and the feelings for my unborn child. It was a rough time because we kept the pregnancy a secret. We both were struggling with our feelings as we continued to try to figure out the best thing to do for our child. You know the rest. But I don't think you know how your mother really felt at that time. I didn't know what she was really going through, because I was too wrapped up in my own feelings. I should've talked more. I should've done a lot of things that I didn't do. I blame myself and…"

Zane threw himself at Jude, sobbing into his chest. "Why didn't she want me?"

That heartbroken question took the breath from Jude's lungs. It burned all the way to his soul and he would remember this moment forever when he would have to account for his decision during that time. And when he would have to account for staying quiet when he should've spoken up. He wrapped his arms around his son and held on with all his strength, trying to convey to him how much he loved him and how much he would always regret that day.

But Jude didn't know if he had enough strength to endure breaking his little boy's heart.

Chapter Eight

"Why didn't she want me?"

Zane wailed into Jude's chest and his heart splintered into jagged sharp pieces that could never be repaired. He held his son, trying to soothe him.

"Shh. Shh," Jude cooed, as if his son were three years old. When his sobs lessened, Jude said, "She did want you. She was just confused about so many things and the counselor gave her some really bad advice. But above everything, she wanted you to have a better life than she ever had. She regretted that decision later."

"She…did?" Zane hiccupped into Jude's chest.

"Yes." He told his son everything Paige had told him. He wanted Zane to know what had happened. "She couldn't get on with her life, because she was grieving for her baby she'd left in Texas."

"You…you came back. Why didn't she?"

"It wasn't that easy for her. She was so far away, struggling to survive when she lost her scholarship and her dorm. It wasn't easy for her to live in a homeless shelter."

Among the horses and the scent of manure and hay, a meaningful silence intruded. Zane sat up and wiped away tears with the backs of his hands. "I don't want to talk about it anymore. I'm sorry for what she went through, but I don't want to see her."

"That's your decision, but I want to point out this might be your only chance to meet your mother."

Zane shook his head. "No. I don't want to."

It wasn't like his son to be so stubborn, but Jude wasn't going to push him. He needed time to adjust to the fact that his mother was nearby.

"Do you know your mother's name?"

"Yes. I looked it up on the computer a long time ago."

"You didn't say anything. I would've told you if you had asked."

"I didn't want you to think I wanted to see her, because I don't. I was just curious."

It was just as Egan had said. Every little boy wanted to know who his mother was and Zane was no exception.

Jude stood. "We better go to the house. Your grandmother is worried."

Zane got up, too, and Jude was reminded that his son wore only his underwear and a T-shirt. He squatted. "Hop on my back. You don't have any shoes on and it's dark."

His son did as instructed and Jude placed his

arms under Zane's legs and walked out of the barn. Zane buried his face in Jude's neck and Jude knew his son was still upset. He hadn't done that in years.

To keep Quincy and Jenny from fretting, Jude knocked on their trailer door and then strolled toward the house. He didn't want to talk, because he knew Zane wasn't ready. He did the same thing at the house, going up the stairs without talking to his mother. She could see that Zane was okay and that was enough. Once Zane was in bed, he'd tell her how he'd reacted.

Zane slid off his back in the bedroom and asked, "Dad, did you get my number for the race?"

Zane seemed to wipe the events of the night from his mind, almost as if they hadn't occurred. He was in denial and Jude would let him get away with that, for now. But he had to face the fact that he had a mother and she wasn't going to go away.

"Yeah. It's in my truck."

"What's my number?" Zane looked at him with big inquisitive eyes and Jude wondered how he could shove all those emotions down inside him. Then he knew. His son was just like him.

"It's twenty-nine."

Zane raised his fist in the air. "I knew it. That's a lucky number for me. Oh, yeah. The race is looking better."

Where was the sobbing boy of a few minutes ago? Jude's head was spinning, but he would leave things alone…for the moment.

"Wash your feet before you get into bed."

"Okay, Dad. Can I go get my number out of your truck?"

"You can get it in the morning. It's time for bed. You have school tomorrow."

A few minutes later Zane was under the covers and Jude stood by his bedside, wondering if he should say something or do something. He wanted to help his son, but he didn't know how. He just didn't want him to be hurt any more than he was. Feeling helpless, he walked toward the door.

"Dad."

He turned back.

"I'm okay."

But Jude knew he wasn't. It was a whole lot of heartache for his little boy and it was going to explode into more heartache than Zane could handle. That was what worried Jude.

"'Night, son."

Jude stood outside Zane's door and knew the heartache extended to him. He now had to tell Paige that her son didn't want to see her.

PAIGE GOT THROUGH the night with the help of her sister and her brother. She didn't understand why she was leaning on them now when

she couldn't before. Back then she'd put up so
many barriers and no one could get through
but Jude. He'd been her whole life, but the Jude
of long ago was no more. He was a man now
and looked at her in an entirely different way.
There was no love, hope or desire in his eyes.
Just a resignation that they shared the connection of a little boy they had created.

The next morning she woke up feeling much
better and stronger. She called Ms. Whitman
to tell her about Zane.

"That's lovely, dear. I'm so happy for you."
Ms. Whitman was in her sixties and loving
and caring to a fault. She had taken in so many
people over the years. Paige had been one of
them.

"Thank you. I'm so excited and worried at
the same time but hopeful that I'll get to meet
my son, my baby."

"I will keep you in my prayers."

"Thank you. Will you do me a favor, please?"

"Anything, dear."

"There's a box in the bottom drawer of my dresser. Would you mind shipping it to me?"

"Sure."

Paige gave her Staci's address and asked that she send it overnight. As she laid her phone on the bed, she missed the warmth and comfort of Ms. Whitman's home. It had saved her from drowning in her own misery.

She then called Dr. Spencer to let her know she would be away longer than two weeks. Dr. Spencer was a well-known doctor in obstetrics and Paige was lucky to get a residency in her medical clinic. She was very understanding, but Paige knew she had to get back to her residency and soon.

After that, she called her friend Thea and told her the good news. Thea advised her to go slow and not to expect too much. Paige thought about that as she dressed and went into the kitchen to join her sister and brother.

Luke and Staci were drinking coffee at the kitchen table. They both looked at her with worried eyes.

She put a French vanilla K-Cup in the Keurig and turned to face them. "I'm fine. Really. I just lost it yesterday, but last night I realized what a gift I've been given. Soon I will see my son. I just have to be patient."

"We've been talking," Luke said as Paige sat at the table. "With everything that has happened, maybe it would be best if we hired someone to paint the house."

"I need something to do while I wait for Jude and I like to paint."

Luke and Staci exchanged glances.

"Don't do that. I'm fine, and a little work will be good for me." She took a sip of her coffee. "Maybe it will exorcise some of those bad memories."

"Let it go, kiddo. I have and I know Luke has. It was bad, but we all got through it and we're all stronger. Now we need to smile and be happy and just enjoy life."

"I'm trying," Paige murmured. But she wondered if the memories would always be there in her dreams. Memories of her mother screaming at her. Memories of scratching her skin until she drew blood. Memories of the nausea churning in her stomach until she threw up. Would they always be there just beyond the realm of happiness, pulling her back?

On the way to Horseshoe, Paige kept her phone in her lap and occasionally touched the screen to see her son's face. It was a small thing, but it would get her through the day.

By midmorning they were busy working. Luke was scraping the trim on the outside of the house and she and Staci were taping the baseboards so they could paint. Staci had chosen a wheat color for the whole house. It would give it a fresh look. Staci had Miranda

Lambert on the iPhone singing away as they wielded the paint rollers over the walls.

Even through the music, Paige heard the knock at the door. She carefully laid her roller in the pan with a trembling hand. "That has to be Jude."

Staci followed suit. "I'll go help Luke scrape to give you some privacy."

Paige took a deep breath and went to the front door. Jude stood there tall and handsome and her heart did a happy dance across her ribs. That wonderful feeling when she saw him hadn't changed. It had been that way since she was seventeen.

"Come in," she said, and walked into the kitchen, queasy from anticipating what Jude was going to say. She turned to face him. "Did you tell him?"

Jude looked down at the hat in his hand. "Yes."

"And…"

He raised his dark eyes to hers and from that one glance her heart fell to the pit of her stomach. "I'm sorry, but he doesn't want to see you."

"No, Jude, please." She'd promised herself she wouldn't cry or lose it again, but the words created another crack in her already shaky emotional facade. Tears trickled from her eyes and she was powerless to stop them or the tremors that ran through her body. She had to get a grip.

"It's his decision and I'm not going to push him."

Tears continued to roll down her face.

"Paige, don't do this. He's twelve years old and dealing with a lot. The fact is he's a lot like me. When he's faced with a difficult situation, he shuts down, but give him time."

"I... I don't blame him, but I was hoping, that's all. I gave him away and I can't expect him to get over that because I'm in town."

"I'm sorry I lost my temper yesterday," Jude said unexpectedly.

She wiped away a tear. "Me, too. Our emotions got the best of us."

"They always did."

"Yeah." She remembered hot kisses and passionate embraces that took them away to a special place with just the two of them. The outside world hadn't mattered. All they'd needed was each other. Feeling weak, she sank into a chair. "Tell me about our son."

Jude took a seat next to her and placed his hat on the table. "As I told you, he's normally a happy kid. One day he's doing all this technical stuff on the computer and the next day he's playing trucks with baby John. He's just a little boy who's dealing with a lot of pain right now. I'll give him a couple of days and then I'll talk to him again. But you have to understand, it's his decision."

She gripped her hands in her lap. "I know. I

would just love to see him. I'm going to stay longer than two weeks and I'm hoping during that time he might change his mind."

"You're staying longer?" There was doubt in Jude's voice.

"Yes. I still can't get over the fact that you've had our son for years."

He shifted nervously. "I'm not going to apologize for that."

"I don't want you to. You did the right thing. Our son is not with the Carstairs but with a big loving family. His real family." How she wished she could be a part of it.

Jude looked around the drab kitchen. "So you're going to do the painting?"

"Yes. I need something to do while I wait for Zane."

"Paige…"

"You don't have to say anything. It's something I have to do for my own peace of mind.

I realize he may never forgive me and—" she stared into his eyes "—you might not, either."

"As two confused teenagers, we did the best we could and I think we both need to move forward now. Your life is in California and mine is here. We're worlds apart, but we have a little boy who needs our utmost attention and patience."

"You really have grown up."

"I had to."

"I believe a lot of the old Jude is still there." She reached out and touched his chest. "Your big heart will never change."

He caught her hand and held it, his calluses rubbing against her soft skin. She remembered that, too. His touch was always so tender and gentle and invited more and more.

"I loved you so much back then." The words were hoarse and seemed to come from deep within him.

"Me, too." She squeezed his hand. "All those

emotions sidetracked us into making bad choices. Or should I say, it sidetracked me into making a bad choice. I can't believe I trusted Mrs. Carstairs."

"No matter what Mrs. Carstairs said, we should have gotten it right, Paige. I should've asked you to marry me and we should have raised Zane together no matter what kind of future was in store for you. That was our obligation as parents and we failed him."

She licked her suddenly dry lips. "Why did you never ask me?"

"I should have. I'm not sure why I never did. But I think I didn't want you to feel trapped like you were with your mother. I wanted you to be free and I thought I could give our son to a loving family and walk away. I couldn't."

"My honorable Jude." She slipped onto his lap and wrapped her arms around his neck and held on for dear life. "I'm sorry I screwed up."

He kissed her cheek and the world stood still

as she felt his skin against hers once again. "We have to stop placing blame. It's over, Paige, and we'll never get those feelings back again."

A pain shot through her as she realized everything she'd lost. Her throat clogged with words and she just kept holding him as if somehow she could instill his warmth into her cold body. But, as he said, their time was over. The sadness of it all still lingered, though.

She slid off his lap with as much dignity as she could manage. "Could you please let me know if Zane changes his mind?"

Jude reached for his hat and got to his feet. "Right now his mind is on the race on Saturday. After that, I'll talk to him again. I'm not promising anything, though."

"I know this is asking a lot, but do you have any pictures that I could look at just to see him as he was growing up?"

He put his hat on his head with a familiar gesture she remembered well, with swagger and bold masculinity. "Yeah, I've taken a bunch over the years. I'll drop them by for you."

"Thank you."

He nodded and walked toward the door and soon she heard him drive away. Polite strangers, that was who they were now. That was more than she'd hoped for.

"Paige."

She swung around to see Staci standing behind her.

"How did it go?"

She swallowed the constriction in her throat. "Zane doesn't want to see me."

"Oh, kiddo, I'm sorry." Staci hugged her and it was a comfort she needed. How could she have stayed away from her sister and brother for so long?

"It's okay. I'm going to keep waiting until I see his face." It was really all she could do now.

"Was…uh…Jude still angry?"

Paige tucked her hair behind her ear. "No. We actually had a nice conversation. Just seeing him brings back so many wonderful times and so many bad ones. It's like I'm balancing on a seesaw. One minute I'm up and the next I'm down. But if I've learned anything in the past thirteen years, it's that we are shaped by the decisions we make. They either make us stronger or we sink into a deep hole of despair. I've been there and I'm not going back. I'm going to fight to see my son and I'm going to continue fighting until Jude forgives me."

"He was there, too, Paige. You're shouldering all the blame and that's not fair."

She slung an arm across Staci's shoulder. "Let's go slick some paint on the wall and turn up the music so we can block out the world." *And my thoughts.* That was what Paige wanted—to not think anymore, to just work until she was tired. Maybe tomorrow or the next day or the next, Jude would come to say that their son wanted to see her. That was what she waited for now. The day her decision would come full circle and she would have to explain to a little boy what an eighteen-year-old girl was thinking at that time. And she prayed she could do it without breaking down.

Chapter Nine

Jude perched on the pipe fence and watched Zane race Bear to the cattle guard, around his mom's house and then all the way to Grandpa's and back to Quincy's barn. As he was watching, he thought of Paige. Over the years he'd managed to push her to the never-never part of his brain, but now she was in present-time reality. And he couldn't deny some of those old feelings were still there. They'd shared a lot and he didn't expect those emotions to just disappear.

Tomorrow he'd try to get some pictures to her. Maybe they would ease her pain. But he would go slow and make sure his heart wasn't involved this time. Once was enough for him.

Zane stopped Bear in front of him. "What do you think, Dad?" His voice was breathless with excitement and his eyes sparkled.

Jude jumped off the fence and rubbed Bear's face. "Very good. How's the saddle working?" Jude had made him a lighter saddle to get rid of some weight.

"Great. I can lean forward on Bear's neck and cut through the wind—" Zane demonstrated, angling his body close to Bear's neck "—like a jockey."

"Bear is sweaty. It's time to rub him down and feed him."

Zane slid from the saddle. "Okay. And, Dad, the protein feed you bought is really working. Bear has a lot more stamina."

Quincy and Jenny were working on the house, so they had the barn to themselves. Zane took care of his horse like an adult. He'd learned to do that early. When he was about three, he'd stand on a bale of hay to brush his horse Venus, otherwise known as Venie. As he grew, he'd wanted a faster horse. His boy loved fast horses.

After removing the saddle, Zane used a hose to cool down Bear. Then he rubbed him with a sponge and a brush. His son was not afraid of work. He'd learned that from Jude. Once the horse was fed and safely in his stall, they headed for the house and supper. Not once did Zane mention his mother. He'd give him another couple of days before bringing Paige up again.

The next morning over breakfast Zane was his usual happy self, talking about the race to his grandmother, Falcon and Quincy. Grandpa and Elias came in and Zane started all over again. Nowhere in his bubbly son was there a sign of sadness, but Jude knew it lurked just below the surface.

A car honked and Zane grabbed his backpack. "Gotta go. Aunt Rachel's here." He usually ran out the door hollering, "Bye, Dad." But today he ran to Jude and hugged him before dashing out. At twelve, Zane had stopped doing the hugging thing except at bedtime. He was a boy and it was embarrassing, Zane had said when he was about eleven.

Jude's brothers and his mom looked at him, but he had nothing to say. He wasn't asking for advice, either. Zane was his son and he would handle the problem. He took his plate and cup to the sink and headed for the back door.

On his way to the office, so many thoughts fought for dominance in his mind. The fact that Zane had hugged him showed that his son was feeling insecure and needed to be close to Jude. And Jude would be there for him every step of the way. Even if it meant standing between him and his mother.

At the office, Falcon talked about what

needed to be done that day. After the rain, they had to wait to get a cutting on the coastal in the south pasture. They had hundreds of acres of coastal that would feed their cattle during the winter months. They sold hay, too. Hay baling would continue during the summer and into September. It was dirty, sweaty work, but their hay was always in high demand.

The brothers saddled up for the day to check the cattle. Jude and Elias went south, while Egan and Quincy rode north. Phoenix and Paxton took the east pastures. Falcon and Jericho went west. The ranch had hundreds of heads of cattle that needed attention on a daily basis.

Jude noted a lot of new baby calves on the ground. Springtime was a time of birth and during roundup they spent days tagging and branding the new ones. A heifer darted out of the bushes and two coyotes were fast on her heels.

Jude turned his horse in that direction and

rode at a quick pace to distract the coyotes. Once the coyotes saw Jude, they sprinted away into the woods. The heifer kept running, frightened. Jude finally saw the cause of the coyotes' interest. A water sac was bulging out of the rear of the heifer. Then he saw two feet. She was having a problem giving birth.

"Elias," he hollered, and drew his rope looped across the saddle horn. He kept pace with the heifer and threw his rope when he was close enough. It landed perfectly over her head and Jude yanked the rope as his horse backed up, holding her tight. Jude dismounted and eased toward the heifer.

"Calm down. No one's going to hurt you. Calm down. That's it." The heifer was breathing heavily and didn't have much strength left. He reached her and stroked her head, talking soothingly. That was when he noticed the heifer's stomach cramping. He'd thought the calf was dead and they would have to pull it.

But she was still in labor. The coyotes had interrupted her.

"Easy. Easy." He removed the rope, knowing the heifer didn't have any energy left for flight.

Elias rode up. "We'll have to pull it."

"No. She's still in labor. Coyotes thought she was an easy defenseless target. I have to get her to lie down."

Elias dismounted. "Good luck with that."

But Mother Nature gave him a hand. The heavy cramps brought the heifer to her knees and she sank to the grass. Jude knelt by her, continuing to speak in soothing tones.

Elias inspected the calf. "This is a done deal. That calf is dead and we have to pull it."

"Just give her a few minutes to calm down. She's still cramping."

"Jude, we have other things to do besides watch this heifer all morning."

Jude raised his head and looked at his impatient brother. "This calf is alive, I'm telling you. Are you gonna help me or are you gonna complain?"

Elias knelt in the grass. "You and Quincy got a double dose of sensitivity."

"Shut up. Your loud voice is disturbing her."

"Well, pardon me."

Jude gave him another look and Elias fell silent.

He could see the calf's feet, still in the same position. All the while, he kept rubbing the heifer and talking softly. "Easy. Easy. Just stay calm. Come on, a couple more pushes." But there was no movement.

"The calf is dead," Elias said again.

"She might need a little help." Jude got to his feet. "Come over here and rub along her back."

"You've got to be kidding. I only rub two-legged females."

"You're an ass." Jude bent down, his boots firmly planted on the ground, reached for the calf's front feet and gently tugged. A nose appeared.

In the meantime, Elias changed his mind and was rubbing the cow, trying to be supportive, which was almost comical. "Okay, this is it. Push."

Almost on cue, the heifer pushed and the calf came out in a big swoosh of water, mucus and blood. Most of it on Jude's boots. He stepped back and watched the wet matted form and waited for it to move. *Please move.*

Elias looked over. "It's dead. I told you."

Jude crouched down and used his gloved fingers to clean mucus out of the calf's nose. After a moment, the calf let out a soft gurgle and Jude glanced at his brother. "Told you."

"Hot damn. That calf is alive."

Jude moved away from the calf and heifer, as did Elias, and let Mother Nature do her thing. The heifer stumbled to her feet and turned around and started to sniff and lick her baby.

After a few minutes, the calf raised its wobbly head and staggered to its feet. Immediately, he started to look for nourishment, nudging his mother's stomach over and over until he found the teats.

Jude and Elias mounted their horses. "After she passes the afterbirth, we have to get them back to the herd," Jude said. "They're too vulnerable out here alone."

"Anything you say," Elias replied with a mock grin.

Jude ignored him, which was the best way to deal with Elias.

Late that afternoon, when he rode back to the barn, he thought about birth and how important it was for the baby to get that first nourishment from his mother and to make a special connection. It cut Jude deeply that his son had missed making immediate contact with the two people who had created him and would continue to love and support him. Every day Jude tried to make up for that.

LUKE FINISHED PAINTING the outside of the house in record time and was ready to head back to Louisiana. Paige hugged him goodbye and held on tight because she knew it would be a long time before she would see her brother again.

"I'll call every time I get a chance," he said. "I hope everything works out for you, sis."

Paige didn't know how anything was going to go, but she knew she was going to miss her brother. "Take care of yourself and stay safe."

He kissed his sisters and walked out the door. They stood for a moment trying not to consider that it might be the last time they would see him. There were no guarantees in war.

She and Staci painted away with the music blaring, both trying not to think. Staci's cell rang and she grabbed it.

"I have to go into work tomorrow. We have a big wedding reception over the weekend and two people have called in sick, so I have to go play catch-up."

"That's okay." Paige put down her brush. "I really need to stay here. Do you think you could drop me in Temple so I can rent a car? That way you don't have to worry about picking me up."

Staci nodded. "I figured you're going to roost here until you see him."

Paige picked up a rag to clean her hands. "That's about it." She wasn't leaving Horseshoe until that moment happened.

An hour later she had a nice little car to drive. On a whim, she stopped at a paint store and bought more paint. Staci had bought enough for only the living room and Paige really wasn't liking the wheat color. She wanted fresh, inviting colors. If she was going to paint the house, she wanted it to look nice, instead of drab and plain.

She picked out a soft yellow for the kitchen, a silky green for her mother's bedroom and a nutmeg for Luke's. She was still undecided about her and Staci's room, but then she found a fresh peach color. It was late when she returned to the house to unload all her purchases. The doorbell rang as she finished carrying everything inside.

Stumbling over paint cans, she sprinted to the door. Jude stood there with a box in his arms and she took a breath to still her racing heart.

"Did Zane change his mind?"

He held up the box. "No, but I brought some photos for you."

She grabbed the box and carried it inside to the living room and sat on the floor. Her fingers trembled as she removed the lid. Jude slid down beside her and she thought nothing could be more perfect than looking at the photos with him.

There were two albums, plus loose photos.

"I put some in albums but got very lazy about that since a lot of photos are on my phone." Jude reached in and pulled out an album and opened it.

Her breath caught as she saw Jude holding a small baby wrapped in a blue blanket. "When did you know we had a boy?" She just had to ask.

"The moment they brought him to me in that blanket."

There were so many beautiful photos of a little boy growing up without a mother that it tore at Paige's heart, but she kept looking, as if by osmosis she could soak up some of that love she should have shared.

"He looks so much like you," she said, touching a photo. "His hair even curls a little."

"Yeah. He inherited a lot of things from me, but there's a lot of you in him, too."

"Like what?"

"Like his intelligence, his curiosity and his need to know more and more about things and the way everything works. Science and the universe intrigue him and he spends hours reading about the planets and stars and everything that makes up this universe. He knows more about the earth than I ever did. He completely blows my mind. That, he gets from you. He's never made a B and he plans to never break that record. I know someone else who used to be like that."

Paige sat cross-legged with the photos in her lap, remembering how important it had been to make all As. Without a 4.0 grade point average, she wouldn't get the scholarship she wanted. That had been the most important thing in the world to her. But looking back, she missed what was really important—all these photos in her lap of a little boy who needed her. Photos without her in them.

Jude scooted back and leaned against the

wall, his long legs outstretched in front of him. "This morning I had to help a heifer have a calf and I thought about Zane's birth. As soon as the calf was on the ground, the heifer stood and sniffed and licked her baby, to let it know she was there to love and to protect it. We weren't there for Zane. We failed him."

A sob rose in her throat and she tried to suppress it but it escaped of its own volition. "You didn't. I…did." Suddenly the photos felt heavy and accusing in her lap.

"I never had the chance to ask, but was it an easy birth?"

Paige pushed down all the guilty feelings, wanting to answer his question. "After they gave me the medication to induce labor, it wasn't long before the cramps started, but they gave me an epidural and it eased considerably. I heard the baby cry and I put my hands over my ears. I didn't understand then why I did that. It was a defense mechanism. I was trying to protect myself. But I've heard that cry for over twelve years and it has haunted me and it has sustained me at times."

"You were so upset afterward I didn't know what to say to you."

"There was nothing you could say. No words, not even from you, could erase the pain that I endured that day." She swallowed a lump that felt like hard clay. "When you took me back to the house to get my things, my mother was in full vitriolic mode. She yelled and screamed as I grabbed my suitcases to leave. She said I would come back with my tail tucked between my legs because I wouldn't last two months in a big-city college. I was a dumb country girl and too stupid to know it. And she wasn't letting me back in the house when that happened. I'd have to find another place to live because she was done raising stupid, ignorant children. That was probably the main reason I never came back. Without my child, there was nothing here for me."

Jude tensed and raised his knees and rested his forearms on them. "How could two teenagers get love so wrong?"

She lifted her eyes to his. "You're the only reason I made it through high school. Luke was in the army and Staci was already living in Austin. After that, home life turned into a nightmare."

Awkwardness crept into the silence and Paige began to put the photos back into the box.

"Are you seeing someone in California?"

A distressed sound left her throat. "I've spent all my time working, going to school, studying and trying to survive. I haven't had time for anything else."

"That's not much of a life."

She carefully placed the lid on the box. "Are you involved with anyone?"

"I've been seeing one of Zane's teachers. She's very good with him and I like her a lot."

She bit her lip, trying to find words that would not make her look like a jealous fool. "Does Zane like her, too?"

He didn't answer her. Instead, he said, "Paige, I'm trying to figure out what's the best thing to do here for Zane. If he continues to refuse to see you, I'm not going to force him."

She wanted to say she understood, but she didn't and her rights as a mother had ended long ago. But she wasn't giving up. Nothing would make her do that now.

"What do you want me to do, Jude?"

His eyes met hers like a dark wall of solid steel that nothing could penetrate. "I want you to leave and never come back."

Chapter Ten

Jude's cruel words pierced the protective barrier she'd built around her heart. All the pain, misery, loneliness and suffering she'd manage to overcome blindsided her, and a renewed pain burned deep inside her. She wanted to cry out from the agony. Her throat closed up and air left her lungs. She didn't need to breathe. She didn't need anything anymore.

Somewhere in that realm of self-pity, the courage that kept her going for so many years resurfaced, saving her.

A barely audible "I can't" came out.

"I know," was his equally quiet response. His

dark eyes held hers captive and she was mes-
merized by the heartache and something else
she remembered well. "And then there's this."
He reached out and ran his hand around her
neck, caressing her sensitive nape, and gentle
waves of comfort flowed through her. It had
been so long.

He pulled her forward, his mouth opening
over hers. She moaned and wrapped her arms
around him, getting as close as possible to return his heated kiss. The box of photos tum-
bled to the floor and neither noticed.

He kissed her as if he was starving for her
taste, her touch, the feel of her. She was the
same, needing to renew every inch of his muscled, firm body. Their lips and tongues did the
talking and they couldn't get enough of the delicious sensation of each other. Locked tight in
his arms, his lips on hers, she thought if she
died like this, she would be a happy woman.
Soon they had to breathe and Jude drew back

slightly, resting his forehead on hers, and she breathed in the scent of him: leather, fresh country air and desire so thick they both recognized it.

"I don't want to hurt Zane and I don't want to hurt you, either." His words were soothing, like a familiar touch in the dark.

"I can't leave." She kissed the spot under his chin and the heat of his skin was a tangible thing that ignited her senses all over again.

"He's already hurting and ignoring his true feelings and I don't know how to help him."

"Just be there for him, but please don't ask me not to see him. Don't punish me. I've paid enough."

Jude got to his feet so quickly she couldn't stop him. Without a backward glance he walked to the door and soon she heard his truck leaving the driveway.

Feeling stunned and overwhelmed, she took a moment to collect her thoughts, trying to figure out what had just happened. He'd kissed her like a man, not a callow youth, but all those emotions were as vibrant as ever and she felt them all the way to her soul. He had to have felt them, too.

The photos were strewn around her. He'd forgotten them. That meant he would have to come back one more time. She gathered the photos like bits and pieces of a giant puzzle, except there was one important piece missing—her.

She touched her aching lips, feeling all his energy once again. How had she survived all these years without him in her life?

Hey, Jude. I still love you.

JUDE DROVE TO the ranch, tired and lonely and looking for answers. He'd been cruel once again to Paige when he hadn't meant to be. Then he'd done what he had wanted to do since the first moment he saw her again at the cemetery—he'd kissed her as if there was no to-morrow. For them there might not be.

Going into the house, he shut off his mind. He was good at that, but today it seemed to hurt a little more than usual. His mom was in the den reading the latest livestock report. She was always up-to-date on the price of cattle.

"Is Zane in his room?"

"Yes. You told him to do his homework and I suppose that's what he's doing. He came down for ice cream about thirty minutes ago and went back up."

"Thanks, Mom." He took the stairs two at a time and found Zane in his room, looking at shirts.

"What do you think, Dad?" Zane held up a white shirt and a red one.

"For school?"

"No, Dad." His son had the nerve to sigh with irritation. "For the race."

"Either will be fine."

"I think the white one. You can see me better in white."

"Okay."

Zane handed it to him. "You have to take it to the cleaners."

"Zane." This time Jude sighed in frustration. "This is Thursday and the race is on Saturday. You should have told me this earlier."

"Mr. Grumby does one-day service."

"But I have a lot of work to do and not a lot of time to run into town and take one shirt and then pick it up."

"Oh. I can ask Aunt Rachel."

"No. I'll figure something out." Zane was his kid and he always took care of his kid. "Have you finished your homework?"

"Does a duck have feathers?"

"You've been talking to Grandpa?"

"Yeah. He knows a lot of stuff. He and Uncle Elias were here earlier and Elias told us how you saved a baby calf today. He said you have more patience than an old maid."

Just what he needed, his son getting barroom quotes from Elias. He stretched his shoulders, realizing how tight his muscles were. He had to loosen up. His time with Paige had him tied up in knots and he needed to do something.

"Time for bed. You have school tomorrow."

"Aw, Dad."

Jude placed his hands on his hips. Zane knew that was a sign his dad wasn't going to give in. He jumped into his bed in his underwear and a T-shirt. That was all he ever slept in. Jude had bought him pajamas because he'd wanted to make sure his kid had all the right things in life. One itty-bitty thing that didn't amount to a hill of beans, as his grandpa would say. Sometimes all a kid needed was love. That was the magic formula.

"Can I stay on my laptop for a few minutes?"

"No, because I know how that goes. Once

you get on there, I can't get you off. No to You-Tube. No to Instagram. Yes to sleep."

"I wanted to post some pictures of Bear, the fastest horse in the West."

A smile threatened Jude's lips. "You can do that tomorrow."

Zane snuggled beneath his Star Wars sheets. "Night, Dad."

He leaned over and kissed his son's forehead. "Night, son."

Suddenly, Zane's arms reached out and hugged Jude tightly around the neck. Jude's stomach cramped at the desperation in those little arms. "Love you, son. Don't ever forget that."

"Love you, too, Dad, and I never forget it."

There was a message in there about his mother, but tonight was not the time to bring it up. That time would be later, when both of them were stronger.

Jude made his way into his bedroom with

years of regret pulling him down into that maze of discontent. He sat on his bed, not bothering to turn on the light. Lying back on the comforter, he closed his eyes and all he could feel was Paige's lips on his, her soft curves pressing into him. All he wanted was to love her the way he had long ago…but that had only brought them misery.

How did they undo all the mistakes? There was no clear answer, just as it had been years ago. Paige's life didn't run parallel with his. She had a career now and he felt deep in his gut there was no room for him or Zane. That was what he couldn't shake.

He knew she regretted her decision about Zane, but where did they go from here?

THE NEXT MORNING Paige was up early and so was Staci. The box from Ms. Whitman had arrived and Paige took it with her to Horseshoe. She was there by eight o'clock. She left it in the car because she wanted it with her if she saw Zane. The box was for him.

With a red kerchief tied around her hair and in jeans and a T-shirt, she started painting the kitchen. The barely yellow color made the room so much fresher and she loved it. She was almost finished when she heard a truck outside. She wiped her hands and ran to the front door.

Jude stood on the doorstep in worn jeans and an equally worn chambray shirt. His hat and boots had also seen better days. He was dressed for work on the ranch. "I forgot the photos last night."

He looked nervous and tense and she was sure the same emotions showed on her face. "They're in the kitchen. I hope you don't mind, but I had some copies made."

"No," he replied as he followed her.

"This looks nice," he said, staring at the new paint.

"Yeah. Wouldn't it be great if we could just paint over all our problems so they would stay hidden for the rest of our lives?"

"Life doesn't work that way."

"I know." She handed him the box. "I wonder how my life would have been if my mother had baked cookies and attended PTO meetings and the only vice she had was putting a little Crown Royal in her Coke."

"That's daydreaming."

"Yeah." She ran her hands down her faded jeans and realized she was making a fool of herself. "Thanks for letting me see the photos. It meant a lot. Do you think Zane is ever going to agree to see me?"

"The race is tomorrow. That's his focus. The thought of you is there, but he's not facing it right now. He will, though. I know my son. He's loving, caring and full of life and he won't avoid the issue of his mother for long."

Jude's words gave her hope.

He carefully placed the box on the table. "I just have to wonder, though, how long you plan on staying in Horseshoe and how he will fit into your life in California."

The hope died with a whimper. "I haven't figured it all out yet. For now I just want to see and hold my son and then I will make decisions for the future. Just don't ask me to leave again."

They stared at each other and the years and the mistakes were clearly pinpointed in their eyes. There was no way to go back. No way to keep daydreaming. No way to go forward but to accept those mistakes as human and move on. And to make sure one little boy wasn't hurt any more than he already was.

As if the topic was getting tedious, Jude quickly changed the subject. "You never said what kind of doctor you are."

"OB-GYN and my specialty is maternal fetal medicine."

"That means you deliver babies?" His face crinkled into an I-can't-believe-this expression.

"Yes. I deliver babies and treat the mothers afterward. It has been the most rewarding experience of my life. With each birth, I feel a renewal of my tattered spirit and when we lose one, I grieve just as I did the day I walked away from mine." She took a long breath. "I'm doing my residency with Dr. Gwyneth Spencer in her medical clinic and she's an amazing teacher and doctor and I have learned so much from her."

"Why did you pick obstetrics?" His face still held the same expression, but it had softened.

"I guess my own experience caused me to have a keen interest in the field and my professors said I had a knack for it. Dr. Spencer said the same thing. She also runs a clinic for pregnant teenage girls and I wished I had had something like that years ago."

"What do you mean?"

"The girls that come there are not judged and they get counseling to help make the right decisions for them and their families. Dr. Spencer has a rule, though. The mother has to hold her baby and say goodbye before she gives it away. She says it's a telling moment. If a young girl can do that without breaking down, then she knows the girl is making the right decision."

His expression softened even more. "Do you think if you had held Zane, you would've changed your mind?"

She eased into a kitchen chair, needing something to hold her up. "I'm almost positive. That's why Mrs. Carstairs didn't want me to see the baby. She knew." She bit her lip, trying to control her anger. "I just needed someone there to talk to and the girls at the clinic get that from Dr. Spencer and her staff."

"I was there. Why couldn't you talk to me?"

She looked into his eyes, loving the way they

crinkled in the corners and loving that everything about Jude was solid and true. Except for one thing: his quietness. "Jude, I don't want to hurt your feelings, but, really, you were more closed up than I was. We didn't do a lot of talking or consoling. If I was upset or if we argued, you'd kiss me and then we'd have sex. That was our problem solver and our *big* problem."

He removed his hat and swiped his hand through his hair. "Yeah."

"Recently we had a fifteen-year-old who gave birth to a little girl. She had already agreed to give it up and her mother was there to support her. The father wasn't in the picture. A couple in their thirties who had been unable to conceive were waiting for the baby. I was with the girl in the room when she held the baby and kissed it goodbye. Some of the things she said to the baby resonated with me."

"Like what?"

"She said she wanted the baby to grow up

with two parents who would love her and they would live in a nice house with a big backyard and she would have everything she wanted. She didn't want the baby to live on welfare like she had. She added the baby would grow up to be a princess because that's what she deserved."

Paige cleared her throat. "I wanted our baby to grow up with the best of everything, too, and I knew that best was not with me in my home environment. By being strong, I felt I was giving him the best. I was so wrong."

"Did you tell the girl that?"

"No. She'd made her decision and she was comfortable with it, but there were lingering doubts, as I'm sure there are with every mother who gives a baby away. When the nurse took the baby, the girl started to cry and she asked if I would hold her. I did. She said she was so cold she was frozen inside. When she said that, I realized I had the same emotions the day I gave birth to Zane. I was frozen inside and I am still. I will never feel any warmth until I'm able to hold my son."

Silence crept over them and Paige grew weary of talking so much about her feelings. Did Jude even understand?

He swallowed visibly. "I'll talk to Zane after the race."

That was more than she had ever hoped for.

Chapter Eleven

Paige painted until midafternoon. She finished the kitchen, the living room and her bedroom. Everything was so fresh and she loved the colors. Her stomach growled and she realized she hadn't eaten anything all day. The morning had been emotional, but music had blocked her thoughts, and physical activity was what she'd needed.

After washing the paint roller, she got in her car and drove to a Dairy Queen and ordered a hamburger, something she would tell her patients to never eat. A healthy diet was the best. But today she felt like being naughty. She ate in the car, not wanting to visit with anyone. Not that anyone would recognize her, but she still wanted privacy.

As she ate, she considered the long drive to Austin every day. Since the house was looking so much better, she thought she might stay there if she had a bed. Downtown had several antiques stores and she drove there. Looking around, she found an old iron bed that she loved. Mr. Jenkins still owned the store and at first he didn't recognize her. After she asked him several questions, his eyes narrowed on her face.

"You're Darlene Wheeler's daughter."

She pushed the strap of her purse farther up her shoulder in a nervous gesture and she hated she couldn't control that. "Yes. I'm Paige."

He bobbed his bald head. "It's nice you've come home. I guess you got a fancy education."

"Yes, sir. I did."

"That's really good." And Paige read the rest of that sentence as *considering who your mother was*. She didn't say anything, because she didn't need to. She knew how the town felt about her mother and there was no way to get around that.

After a few minutes of talking back and forth, she bought the bed and asked about mattresses. He said he had some in the back in case people needed them. To get there she had to go through a maze of tables, furniture, bric-a-brac and everything known to man, even a toilet. Who would buy a toilet in an antiques store?

In the far back he had two sets of mattresses wrapped in plastic. "A fella passed through here and wanted to know if I was interested in mattresses. I bought four and I still have two." He pointed. "Your choice."

She bought one to fit the iron bed and Mr. Jenkins said he could deliver it out in the late afternoon. After that, she drove to Temple and bought towels, sheets, a microwave and a coffeepot. She also bought a few groceries. Then she called Staci.

"You're not serious."

"I want to be in Horseshoe if Zane decides to see me. The house is looking really nice. The new colors made a world of difference."

"Kiddo, don't get your hopes up. I'm afraid you're going to get hurt again."

"I have to see this through, even if it takes forever."

There was silence on the other end for a moment. "When will I see you?"

"Tonight. I have to get my things. And don't be all sad sack. You work all the time and I would just be sitting in your apartment."

"Yeah, I'm sorry about that."

"When you get some spare time, you can come spend the night with me in the house. It will be like old times."

"Pleeeease. Old times I do not want to re-live."

Paige laughed and it was great to find humor in their terrible childhood. "I'll see you tonight."

When she pulled into her driveway, Mr. Jenkins drove in behind her. A teenage boy helped him and within fifteen minutes they had the bed and mattress set up.

"Nice seeing you, Ms. Wheeler." He tipped his baseball cap to her.

"Thank you, Mr. Jenkins." Nothing else was said and Paige was grateful he didn't ask a lot of questions.

She put away all the stuff she'd brought and then made the bed, placing the old worn teddy bear in the center. Blinds were still on the windows, so she didn't have to worry about anyone peeping in. She glanced at her handiwork and even though it wasn't stylish, it would do.

It was crisp and clean and would be all she needed as she waited for her son.

Saturday morning dawned bright and early. Too early for Jude. Zane woke him up at ten to five and Jude pulled him into the bed and pretended to smother him with a pillow. Zane laughed and squirmed and they roughhoused as they often had when he was little.

"Come on, Dad. You have to get up. It's Saturday." Zane wiggled out of his arms and off the bed and stood there smiling with his hair in his eyes. No one would know his little heart was breaking.

Jude swung his legs over the side of the bed and sat up. "The race isn't until two."

"But we're having lunch there and everything. The whole town will be there to celebrate Founder's Day. We have to get there early so I can walk Bear around and he can get used to everything. You know he's kind of fidgety and nervous. I want him to be relaxed."

Jude reached out and caught his son's arm and pulled him down beside him. "I'm glad you're so excited about this, but we need to have the talk about winning and losing."

"Aw, Dad, we've had that talk. Winning is great, but there's no shame in losing." Eyes as dark as Jude's glanced at him. "Do you think I'm going to lose?"

"No, son, but I'm proud of you whether you win or lose and so is everyone in the family. Sometimes, though, you have to be prepared for both."

"I am, Dad."

"I'm also proud of all the energy and effort you've put into making Bear a faster horse. That shows maturity and it shows me how important this is to you."

Zane frowned. "Don't get mushy."

Jude hugged his son. "That would be terrible."

"Yes." Zane jumped up and slid across the hardwood floor in his socks and underwear and it reminded Jude of an old Tom Cruise movie. "We gonna have a par-ty," Zane sang.

Jude wished Paige could see her son like this, all happy and excited with no worries in the world. After talking to Paige yesterday, Jude couldn't get her and all the pain she'd suffered over the years out of his mind. He'd never dreamed her life had been like that. He would talk to Zane on Sunday about his mother and make him listen. He had to face the fact that he had a mother and they needed to meet. It wasn't going to be easy, but he had to do it. It was the right thing to do for all of them.

"Dad, you have to wear a white shirt today."

Zane brought him out of his thoughts. "Why?"

"Because we're all wearing white shirts."

"Who's all?"

"The Rebel family." Zane dragged the words

out slowly, as if his father might have a hard time grasping the fact.

"And whose idea was this?"

Zane thumbed into his chest. "Mine. Everyone on Team Zane is wearing a white shirt. Erin and Jody are wearing white and some other kids."

Erin was the DA's daughter and Jody was the sheriff's daughter. They were older than Zane, but because Zane had been moved up a grade, they were now in the same classes and had become friends.

"Well, then, I better find a white shirt, because I'm definitely on Team Zane."

The morning turned into a circus with Zane buzzing around like a pesky mosquito, annoying everybody. He was just so excited he couldn't calm down. He insisted on washing Bear and brushing his tail and mane so he would look beautiful. Jude finally sat him down and made Zane take a couple of deep breaths.

Paige had been just like that in school over tests and school activities she was involved in. She'd get all excited and break out in a rash and she'd cry and get overemotional. Her son was just like her. He panicked easily, except he rarely cried.

Finally, they made their way to the fair-grounds with Bear in the horse trailer. Jude's mother and Phoenix rode with them to help calm Zane. The fairgrounds were three blocks off Main Street. The land had been donated by Delbert Miller, whose ancestors had been one of the town's founding families back in the 1800s. He'd willed twenty-five acres and a house to the town of Horseshoe. The house had been redone and it was now used for weddings, parties, reunions and things like that. The race started at the house and went around the property and back. It was for kids nine to eighteen and all the Rebel boys had raced over the years, as every kid in Horseshoe had.

Bubba Wisnowski and his friends always set up a barbecue stand at the event. Usually everyone brought food, but the barbecue was the big deal. There were games and fun activities for all the kids. The Rebel family gathered beneath a big live oak tree by the house and everyone wore white shirts. Zane was happy.

His mother had brought fried chicken and the others contributed potato salad and sweets. They settled on quilts and ate lunch. There were a few chairs, occupied mostly by the women and Grandpa. Being pregnant, Rachel took a chair. Egan teased her that he'd never be able to get her up off the ground. They laughed and savored a spring afternoon with family.

Zane talked incessantly and Jude had to make him stop. He was nervous—that was very evident. The McCray family gathered on the other side of the house and Jude watched as Malachi McCray unloaded Dudley's horse. She was a brown mare with a blaze on her face and long legs. Just by looking at the horse, Jude could tell she was fast. A grain of doubt lay on his conscience and he knew his son had his work cut out for him to beat that horse.

The mayor gave a speech, as did Judge Hollister. Then everyone visited and talked and enjoyed the day.

"Fifteen minutes to race time," Wyatt, the sheriff, announced over the loudspeakers.

"Don't forget to watch me," Zane shouted to the family, and ran to the trailer where Bear was waiting. Jude and Quincy followed more slowly.

"Tuck your shirt in," Jude said. Zane's shirt was hanging out of his pants and there was a stain on it, but he didn't point that out. Ever since he was a little boy, Zane couldn't keep a white shirt clean more than fifteen minutes.

Jude should have remembered that when Zane had asked about the shirts.

"Now, remember, partner, stay calm and focused and Bear will do the rest." Quincy was talking to Zane.

Jude pinned Zane's number on the back of his shirt.

"My lucky number."

Jude wanted to hug his son, but he didn't, because he knew that would embarrass him. "You can do this. You've worked hard and you can ride that horse to victory."

"Thanks, Dad." Zane, for the first time today, seemed to calm down. He put his foot in the stirrup and swung into the saddle. He rode to the starting line without another word.

His son looked so much older atop the horse, sitting in the saddle like a pro. And Jude stood there staring after him, wishing Zane's mother could see him now.

PAIGE SAT AT the kitchen table eating a salad and wondered how the race was going. She picked at the salad and then threw it into the garbage. Her nerves were tied into knots and she had to get back to painting. It would take her mind off the race. But that didn't help. She wanted to see her son. Jude hadn't invited her and she didn't want to go and cause a scene. But she wanted to see him so badly.

Ten minutes later she was in her car and driving into town. Nothing looked to be open, because everyone was at the fairgrounds, but she was hoping Mr. Jenkins's antiques shop was. She'd seen some old hats in his place yesterday and one of those was just what she needed to disguise herself. Her luck held. Mr. Jenkins was in front sitting in a rocking chair, watching the town. Usually several merchants stayed behind to keep an eye on things because even in Horseshoe there were thieves.

She bought a big floppy hat that tied beneath

her chin and made her way to the fairgrounds. Her car was small, so she was able to find a parking spot near the starting line. Riders on horses were milling around waiting for a signal. She could see clearly, so there was no need to get out.

Her eyes scanned the riders and then she saw him on a paint horse wearing a white shirt. No one had to point him out. Her son was a clone of his father. She stared, soaking up every little detail. He was thin, which he must've gotten from Jude, too, because Paige had never been thin until grief had killed her appetite.

He was so handsome she couldn't look away. He handled the horse expertly and guided him to the starting line. Most of Horseshoe was here today, but only one person held her attention. It might have been wrong for her to be there, but she was going to watch her son win this race.

JUDE FROWNED AS the boys lined up. Zane was on the right and Dudley on the left. The other racers were in between. Jude didn't like that positioning and he wished he'd talked to Zane about that, but it was too late. He felt Zane was going to get crowded out. Now Jude was nervous.

Wyatt spoke to the boys and told them the rules. Then he stepped back and everyone waited eagerly. The Rebel family stood together, their attention on the race. Even baby John stopped toddling around, as if he knew something important was about to happen.

Wyatt pulled his revolver from his holster and pointed it toward the sky. On the count of three, he fired. The thunder of hooves echoed and the race was on.

Just as Jude feared, Zane was pushed to the side, but he made up time quickly. The race went around the property and was more like an obstacle course as it went uphill and then down through Yaupon Creek. The riders were soon out of sight but Jude caught a glimpse every now and then through the mesquite and the oaks. But he had no idea who was leading the race.

Quincy slapped him on the back. "Stop worrying. Zane has this."

"He was just so excited about it and I don't want him to be disappointed."

"He's not." Phoenix joined the conversation. "He's the best rider out there."

They saw the dust billowing before they saw the riders. Zane and Dudley were out front, neck and neck, racing toward the finish line. But something was wrong. Zane wasn't straight in the saddle as Jude had taught him. He'd leaned slightly and that wasn't like his son at all.

"Here they come!" Grandpa shouted. "There's Zane right in front. Come on, boy!"

"Something's wrong," Jude muttered.

The Rebel brothers gathered around him. "Zane's leaning," Falcon said.

"I know." Jude moved toward the finish line and watched as his son suddenly leaned forward and Bear, with a burst of energy, shot away from Dudley. By the time Zane crossed the finish line, he was ahead by two links. But Bear kept running. Zane didn't pull him up and there had to be a reason for that.

Jude took off running for his son and looked on in horror as Zane slipped from the saddle to the ground, one boot caught in the stirrup. When that happened, Bear finally stopped and Zane was dragged only a few feet. Jude fell down by his limp son and stared at the blood on his face and shirt. Fear climbed inside him and held his heart in a vise.

Quincy grabbed Bear's reins and Phoenix gently removed Zane's foot from the stirrup. His other brothers had reached them by then and they knelt as Jude half lifted Zane into his arms, carefully cradling his head.

"What the hell happened?" Elias asked.

There was a cut on Zane's forehead and it was bleeding. The left sleeve of his shirt was shredded and it was caked with more blood.

"Zane," Jude called, and had to clear his throat as his emotions twisted into a painful knot. "Zane, son, wake up." But Zane lay still, unmoving, and the bright sunshiny day full of hope turned into a nightmare.

"Get Jenny!" Jude shouted. She was a nurse and would know what to do. But someone else pushed in beside him and he didn't have to look to know who it was.

Paige.

Chapter Twelve

"Get some towels and water," Paige ordered.

Jenny crouched down beside her with the items. Paige took a towel and pressed it against the cut on Zane's forehead. "We have to stop the bleeding first. Hold it while I examine the other cuts."

Jude just watched as Paige dealt with their injured son. She undid the buttons on his shirt and removed it so she could see Zane's arm. "Another bleeder on his neck. We're lucky it missed the main artery." She applied another towel to his neck and held it.

"There's so much blood," Jude said.

"The are many blood vessels on the face and skull, and once the skin is broken, it tends to bleed excessively. Hopefully, we can stop it with pressure." She glanced at Jude then. "Remove his boots to see if his ankle is swelling from getting caught in the stirrup."

Her voice was firm, in control. This wasn't the anxious girl he'd known. This was a professional doctor.

He quickly stripped off Zane's boots and socks. "There's a slight bruise, but it's not swelling—yet."

"Good. He'll need an X-ray." She continued to look at Zane's arm. "Slashes have broken through the epidermis and the cuts look superficial, but I'm worried about his head hitting the ground. And it looks as if someone has beaten him with something."

Jude looked up and saw Dudley still on his horse holding a riding crop. Rage filled Jude. He got to his feet and marched to Dudley, who didn't have enough sense to ride away. Reaching up, he grabbed him by the collar and pulled him out of the saddle and onto the ground. Dudley tried to hit him with the crop, but Jude jerked it out of his hand and pressed his boot down on Dudley's throat.

"I'm going to show you what it feels like to be whipped!" He pushed his boot down harder and the boy gasped for breath.

"Jude," Quincy called. "Don't do this."

"Look at Zane and tell me not to do this. I'm going to teach this piece of crap a lesson." He leaned even harder on his foot and the boy started to turn blue.

"Jude, Zane's going to be okay. This isn't worth it." Quincy kept up his plea.

"Do something," Malachi said to Wyatt, who had finally made it to the scene.

"Let him up," the sheriff ordered. "I'll take care of this."

"Daddy." A little voice, Zane's voice, came

out of nowhere and brought Jude to his senses. He was hurting a kid. He let up the pressure on Dudley's neck. "Tell me why you hurt Zane."

The boy coughed but didn't say anything. Jude pushed his boot down again and Dudley moaned, "O-kay."

"Why did you beat Zane with the crop?"

"Dad…Dad…said…if I didn't win…he'd beat me."

Jude looked at Malachi and all the years of the Rebels and McCrays fighting seemed to escalate in that moment. He threw the crop at Malachi and it bounced off his chest to the ground. Jude walked away to his son without another word.

Over his shoulder he saw Jericho pick up the crop and poke it into Malachi's chest. "You better watch your back."

"He's threatening me," Malachi told the sheriff.

Egan pulled Jericho away.

"You have a lot more to worry about than Jericho," the sheriff said. "I'm taking Dudley to the jail and you and your wife had better be in my office in thirty minutes."

Jude knelt once again by his son, who was now awake, and took a second to let the anger subside.

"Dad-dy, did…I win?" Zane asked.

"You bet you did."

"I want…my trophy."

"He needs to go to an emergency room," Paige said. "Keep something under his head and keep him awake. Make sure they do a CT scan of his head. And he needs a tetanus shot if he hasn't had one."

"Maybe you should come with us," Jude said.

Zane glared at Paige and cried, "No, Daddy." Zane never called him Daddy unless he was upset. "I want Aunt Jenny to come with us."

"I'm right here, sweetie." Jenny kissed the top of Zane's head.

Paige seemed undeterred by her son's outburst. A large purse was beside her and she pulled something out of it.

"The bleeding has stopped," Jenny said.

"Good." Paige poured some water over a towel and dabbed at the cut on Zane's forehead. "This is an alcohol wipe. I'm going to clean the cuts and apply some surgical strips. This might sting a little." She thoroughly cleaned the cut on his forehead and the one on his neck and applied the strips with the utmost care and concentration. Zane frowned and winced but didn't say another word.

"This will keep the cuts from opening again and maybe you won't have to have stitches or much of a scar." She sat back on her heels. "That should do it. Remember to keep his head supported at all times until you reach the ER."

"Daddy, what about Bear?"

"Don't worry about Bear," Paxton told him. "I'll take him back to the ranch."

"Is he hurt?"

"Nah. Bear's tough." They really hadn't looked at the horse yet and Jude was grateful that Paxton had gone with his gut on the answer.

The whole family had gathered around. Even Jude's mother and Rachel were kneeling on the ground beside Zane. Falcon had a close hold on Grandpa, who had a shattered look on his face.

Kate held Zane's hand and Jude could see tears in her eyes. Egan helped Rachel to her feet and she buried her face in his chest so Zane couldn't see her cry.

Quincy drove his truck up as close as possible and Jude lifted his son, with Jenny holding towels under his neck, and put him in the backseat.

"We'll meet you at the hospital," Egan called.

"No," Jude shouted back. "That's not necessary. Meet us at the house and we're still going to have that party to celebrate like we planned."

In a few seconds they roared away with Phoenix in the passenger seat. Jude looked back to see Paige standing alone. People were walking away, even his family. He should have insisted that she come, but he couldn't. He was caught between his son and his son's mother.

PAIGE WAS FROZEN in place. She couldn't seem to move or do anything but feel the pain in her chest. Then her body started to tremble and she knew the reaction was starting. Wrapping her arms around her waist, she tried to control her emotions. She'd touched her son and braved the anger in his eyes. She hadn't expected anything less but, oh, it hurt. She felt as if someone had reached in and pulled out her heart. She gasped for air.

She'd been patiently waiting for the riders to make the turn and then she saw Zane and the other boy neck and neck, racing toward the finish line. She'd shouted out loud when Zane crossed the line first. But then Jude had started to run toward their son and she'd known something was wrong. To her horror, Zane fell from the saddle, and she quickly grabbed the small medical bag she always kept with her and dashed over to them. She hadn't even stopped to think that Zane would not want to see her. He was hurt and she would not let her pride or his anger keep her from helping him.

She was still reeling from the fact that the boy had whipped her son like an animal. The feud between the Rebels and McCrays was still as crazy as ever. So much hate. So much bitterness. Would it ever end?

"Paige."

She'd been so locked within herself she hadn't even realized that Rachel had come back and now stood by her side.

"Are you okay?"

She tucked strands of hair behind her ear and felt a cool breeze on her face. The tightness in her lungs eased and she noticed that people were packing up for the day, loading horses and picking up trash. A sad ending to Founder's Day.

"No. I don't think I'll ever be okay again." And then she looked into Rachel's eyes. "You know, don't you?"

"Yes."

"How many other people know?"

"Just the Rebel family, I think. Egan told me and I would never betray his confidence. I haven't told a soul."

"Not even Angie?"

"Not even Angie."

Paige sucked air into her burning chest. "I made a huge mistake and I don't know how to make it better. I don't know how to explain it to my son. I don't even know how to explain it to myself."

Rachel put her arm around Paige and hugged her. "We all make mistakes, Paige."

"But not like the one I made."

"It may surprise you, but people can be very understanding."

"And very cruel. I remember that from high school."

"You had a horrid childhood and everyone in this town knows that. No one blames you." She squeezed Paige's shoulder. "Stop blaming yourself. You were amazing with Zane. You were always a cut above the rest of us in school and it showed today. You have an amazing talent and I'm glad you got the education you wanted. Yes, it came with a price, but I'm betting Jude and Zane will feel the same way I do. Just give them time."

Paige choked back a sob and hugged her friend. She'd never expected anyone to be this generous and kind and it brought tears to her eyes.

They pulled apart and Rachel said, "You know, mistakes are like marks on a chalkboard. With a little effort and patience, they can be erased."

Paige smiled through her tears. "I don't know if I have an eraser that big."

"All it takes is love." Rachel touched her forehead. "My hormones are a little crazy right now, but I firmly believe you, Jude and Zane should be together."

"Honey," Egan called.

"Coming!" Rachel shouted back. "Call me if you need to talk."

"Thank you."

Rachel walked off toward Egan, and Paige made her way to her car. If not for Rachel's kind nature, Paige would probably have been crying her eyes out right now. That tiny spark of hope in her chest burned a little brighter.

She went back to her painting job, but she'd lost interest. She kept wondering how Zane was. Jude had her phone number and she was hoping he would call. By late afternoon the phone still hadn't rung and she knew Jude wasn't going to call. So that meant she had to make a big decision: whether to see her son or not.

JENNY CALLED AHEAD to the emergency room and two orderlies were waiting with a stretcher when Quincy pulled in. Zane had a death grip on Jude's hand and wouldn't let go.

"It's okay, son. They have to get you out of the truck. It will only be for a few minutes. I'm not going anywhere."

Zane released his hand and the orderlies had him out in seconds and on the stretcher. Things happened fast after that. The ER doctor examined him and said he wouldn't disturb the surgical strips that someone had put on, because they had been done so expertly and the wound was already closing. Then they spent hours doing tests and Zane was nervous, but Jude never left his side. He was always near and Zane knew that.

By late afternoon they got the okay to go home. Zane was fine, just a little bruised. There was no swelling or bleeding of the brain.

Jude phoned the family to let them know they were on the way. The moment he opened the front door, everyone shouted, "Congratulations!" There were balloons, streamers and a banner that Eden and Leah had made. Cake and punch were on the dining room table and Zane was all smiles. The smile got even wider when he saw the trophy sitting next to the cake.

Falcon handed it to him. "Hardy brought this by and said to tell you congratulations."

"Wow! Look, Dad. It's so big."

He hugged his son. "I'm proud of you, but we have to get you upstairs to change your clothes." Zane's shirt was ruined and it had been left at the fairgrounds and Jude was sure someone had thrown it away. He had a hospital gown on and his jeans. That was it. They had wrapped his ankle to keep it from swelling and Jude had to keep a close eye on it. Zane limped slightly and the doctor had said for him to stay off that foot as much as possible for the next few days. That might be a problem.

Jude brought him down in his pajamas. He'd known one day those things would come in handy. Zane sat on the sofa with the trophy in the crook of his arm. His grandmother brought him cake and punch and he was the center of attention, but Jude noticed the fear that was still in his son and probably would be for days to come.

There was a knock at the door and no one seemed to hear it, so he left his son in good hands and went to answer it. Paige stood there looking a little nervous.

"I'm sorry to intrude, but I have to know how he's doing."

Seeing the worry in her green eyes, Jude made a decision. It was time for Zane to talk to his mother. It might not be the best time, but Jude was going with his gut feeling.

He opened the door wider. "Come in. But be prepared for some attitude."

"I can handle it."

Jude felt that she could. She wasn't a shy, insecure teenager anymore.

The room fell silent as they walked in. Zane's eyes grew huge and he glanced down at the trophy in the crook of his arm, refusing to look at his mother.

His mom came forward and held out her hand. "Thanks for what you did for Zane today."

"You're welcome." The words came out low but they heard them.

Jude motioned behind Paige for everyone to go into the kitchen. His brothers and their fam-

ilies slowly got up and made an exit, followed by his mother and grandpa.

Zane looked nervously around. "No, come back."

Jude walked over and sat on the coffee table facing his son. "I want you to do something for me."

"What?" Zane spoke into his chest, not raising his head.

"Look at me."

Zane raised his head and Jude saw two black orbs of anger staring back at him.

"I want you to talk to your mother and tell her everything you're feeling. Tell her all the anger and resentment inside you. Let it all out, and then if you never want to see her again, you don't have to. It's that simple, son. You have to do this. I've never forced you to do anything, but today I'm asking you to talk to your mother and let her know exactly how you feel." He got up and went into the kitchen to join the family, but he kept his ear to the door. If his son needed him, he wanted to be there. The rest of their lives depended on what Zane said now.

PAIGE GAVE ZANE a few minutes and then she walked over and perched on the coffee table where Jude had sat, facing her very angry son. Confronting her mistakes was harder than she'd ever imagined. The urge to leave was strong, but she owed this little boy an explanation and he was going to get it, even if it took a piece of her soul.

"Your color is much better. How do you feel?"

"Go away and leave me alone," Zane spat into his chest.

"I can't do that. I've waited for years to see what you look like and this moment surpasses anything that I've ever imagined. A day has not gone by that I haven't thought of you. I hoped you were with a loving family who cared for you and gave you everything that I couldn't."

"My daddy gave me everything I needed because he loves me."

"He's a special kind of man and I've always known that."

There was silence for a moment, a silence that was pressing into her lungs, leaving her breathless.

"I love you, too."

His dark eyes finally lifted. Paige felt a chill like nothing she'd ever felt before.

"Then why did you give me away?"

"I was young and naive, dealing with a lot of emotional upset at home. My one goal was to leave Horseshoe and my mother and never come back. I could try to explain it and make myself look good, but the honest truth is I was just a scared teenager unsure about myself and the future and the child I was carrying. I so badly wanted you to have a better life than I ever had."

"That's just an excuse."

Paige reached into her big bag and pulled out the box she'd been saving all these years for him. She leaned over and placed the box beside him. "When I was about three months pregnant, I started reading to you. I had to do it in the bathtub, where my mother couldn't hear or see me. I read the books over and over to you and I wrote messages in each one for you. I meant to give them to the adoptive parents, but somehow in the emotional upheaval, I forgot. I saved them all these years. So if you want to know what I was feeling at that time, those books will tell you."

"I don't want them."

She swallowed hard, trying not to let his words derail her. "You can throw them away, then, but you'll never know how hard it was for me to give you away."

"Why did you come back? We don't want you here."

"My mother passed away and I came for the funeral and your father gave me this amazing gift. He had my baby, my precious baby, who I had been grieving for all these years."

"No, you weren't. You went on with your life, got an education and became a doctor. You didn't want a baby. That's why you got rid of me."

A sob blocked her breathing and it took a moment for her to gather her courage once again. "I don't know what else to say to you to ease your pain, but I love you and I can't tell you what a joy it was when your father told me he had you, and then to see your beautiful face for the first time was an incredible high."

"I wish you'd never seen me."

"Then I would've died a lonely and miserable woman."

"Good. I hope you leave and never come back."

Paige felt like a boxer in a ring, taking hit after hit and still having the stamina to keep fighting. But her strength was waning. She couldn't continue to do this to him or to her. It was too painful.

She got to her feet. "Maybe one day you'll open the box and maybe one day you'll open your heart and realize that life is full of decisions and sometimes we make the wrong ones. But we're blessed with an amazing ability to forgive. My hope for us is that we'll be able to do that in the future. Goodbye, my precious son."

Chapter Thirteen

Jude wanted to go after Paige, but his son whimpering like a little puppy on the sofa stopped him in his tracks. The choices Jude and Paige had made years ago were tearing their son apart and Jude felt the weight of that like a mantle of solid steel on his shoulders.

After the emotional day, Zane wasn't ready to talk to his mother. Now Jude had to deal with the aftermath. He picked up his son as if he was three years old and carried him upstairs to his bed and tucked him in.

"Daddy." Zane hiccupped.

"What, son?"

"My head hurts."

He wanted to say so many things, but once again his son had retreated into himself, blocking out the pain, blocking out his mother. It was a trait he'd inherited from his father.

Jude glanced toward Quincy and Phoenix, who lingered in the doorway with worried expressions. "Would you get the prescription we picked up at the drugstore?"

Phoenix turned and went downstairs to do as asked, but Quincy came farther into the room. "Can I speak to him for a minute?"

"Quincy—" Jude could take care of his own son and he didn't want anyone interfering, not even Quincy. But then he realized that he was being a little touchy. Zane loved Quincy, so Jude stepped aside and motioned for his brother to come forward.

Quincy squatted by the bed. "Hey, partner. You did great today and I'm so proud of you."

Zane just lay with his head on the pillow, reminding Jude of a broken doll, unable to communicate.

"Don't worry about Bear. I checked him over and he's fine. He's fed and in his stall for the night."

"Thank you, Uncle Quincy."

Quincy brushed hair from Zane's forehead. "Get some rest and I'll see you tomorrow."

Phoenix came back with the medication and a glass of water. Jude gave Zane a pill. "This will ease the pain in your head and help you to rest."

Zane took it without a word and curled into a ball in the bed. The sight did a number on Jude's control. The last thing he wanted was for his son to get hurt.

Jude's mother came into the room and he knew he had to put a stop to all the family togetherness. He and Zane had to deal with this alone. But he would never be rude to his mother.

"I just want to say good-night," Kate said, kissing Zane's forehead. "Good night, my precious baby."

"Don't call me that," Zane snapped, and Jude moved toward the bed. Zane had never been disrespectful to his grandmother and Jude wouldn't allow it, either.

"Zane."

"I'm sorry." Then he started to cry and Jude gestured for everyone to leave the room.

Jude sat on the bed and gave his son a minute. "I know you're hurting, but sometimes we have to feel the pain before we can feel the joy. I'm here to help you and I love you. So many people love you."

"I don't want to see her again."

Jude swallowed, knowing a line had been drawn and he had to honor what he'd told his son. He wouldn't force him to see or talk to Paige again. "Okay." He pulled the Star Wars sheets over Zane and kissed his cheek. "Good night."

"Dad-dy." The name was drawn out and Jude knew his son was drifting into sleep. Jude sat with him until he was sound asleep.

Slowly, Jude went into his room and stopped short when he saw Phoenix lying on the bed. He sat up when he noticed Jude.

"How's the kid?"

"Not good." He ran a hand through his hair. "I shouldn't have forced it. It was too soon, but I thought…"

"It's been a rough day. Don't beat yourself up. Tomorrow everything will be better."

"I don't know, Phoenix. I've never seen Zane this upset."

"I know absolutely nothing about kids, but I've been told that they're tough. And Zane's a tough little kid. Dudley tried to knock him out of the saddle, but Zane kept holding on, refusing to give up. I think that says something about his character. He's mad at his mother. He made that abundantly clear. My guess is that will pass. You just have to give him time."

"She was so hurt by his words."

"Yeah, but she had to have known it wouldn't be a picnic."

"She said she was prepared, but how do you prepare for something like that?" Jude had been peeping around the door, just in case Zane needed him, and he'd seen the shattered look on Paige's face. She hadn't been prepared at all.

"Can you stay here for a little while?"

"Um…I guess. Why?"

"I have to make sure she's okay."

Phoenix groaned. "Jude, don't do this. You barely survived the first time and now you're jumping right back…"

"Zane should sleep for a while. I won't be gone long. Call me if he even stirs. Just don't leave him alone."

Phoenix lay back on the bed and reached for the remote control. "Okay, but you better get your butt back here in a hurry."

Jude was out of the house in five minutes. His mother was in her room, so he didn't have to explain anything. Everyone else had gone to their own homes. It was like living in a fish-bowl.

It didn't take him long to make it to Paige's house. He was just hoping she hadn't driven back to Austin. A car was in the driveway and the house was dark. The car wasn't Staci's, so Paige must have rented one. That puzzled him. Was she staying in the house?

He wasn't sure what he was doing here. He thought she might need comforting after the talk with Zane, but clearly she had gone to bed or had left with Staci. He'd worried for nothing. Then it hit him. He was repeating an old pattern of comforting Paige. So many times he'd come here when her mother had been so vile to her. But Paige didn't need him anymore. It was about time he faced that. Even though he was still attracted to her, she had moved on to the life she'd wanted without him. But those old habits still died hard.

PAIGE DIDN'T BOTHER with the lights in the house. She went straight to her bedroom and cried as though her whole world was crashing down around her, and in a way, it had. Her son's anger destroyed all her confidence and made her weak because he had that much power. He had every right to say what he wanted. She just hadn't been prepared for the pain.

The sound of a door opening had her sitting up straight. She hadn't locked the door, but this was Horseshoe and she felt safe. She got out of bed and tiptoed to the doorway and down the hall. She could see a figure, a tall dark figure, standing near and her heart leaped into her throat.

"Paige."

She sagged against the wall at the sound of the voice that was dear to her. *Jude.*

"I'm in the bedroom." She went back and sat on the bed, waiting for him.

"Why are there no lights on?"

"Because I like the dark. In the light, I can see all my flaws and there are many."

His shadowy figure framed the doorway. "Well, it's hard to see. Are you living here now?"

"Yes. With the new paint and all, it looks so much better and I wanted to be near in case Zane…you know…"

"Yeah." He moved farther into the room.

"Why are you here and not with Zane?"

He sat on the bed beside her and it sagged, drawing them closer. "His head was hurting, so I gave him a pill the doctor prescribed and he's out for the night. I was worried about you."

"What if he wakes up?"

"Phoenix is with him. How are you?"

"I've cried until I can't cry anymore. Now I'm just numb. I knew it would be hard, but I never imagined it would hurt this bad. It hurts."

He put his arm around her and she rested her head on his shoulder, loving his strength and his softness at the same time. There was no one like Jude, with his big heart and his code of honor. That was why she never minded too much when he was quiet. She knew she could trust and depend on him no matter what.

"I'm sorry." He kissed her hair and his lips trailed to her cheek, to her jaw and then to the corner of her mouth. She touched his face and felt the stubble of his beard and breathed in the scent of him, which, oddly, smelled like birthday cake.

"You've been eating cake."

"Mmm. Mom baked a celebration cake for Zane."

"Jude." She buried her face into his chest and

burrowed against him, trying to get as far away from herself as she could. If she could soak up one ounce of goodness from him, maybe she could breathe normally again.

His arms went around her and he held her, rocking her gently, and her feelings for him were as new and vibrant as they'd ever been. "We've made mistakes, Paige, and it's time to stop paying for them. It's time to start living."

"It just kills me that he's hurting."

"Shh." His lips touched hers and it was like striking a match. Every sense ignited and all she wanted was him. Completely and forever. His mouth opened over hers, their tongues tasted and danced, and they took and gave until they were breathless with need. Time and place ceased to exist. It was just them, two teenagers or two adults. It didn't matter. It was all the same because it was Jude and Paige and it would always be that way.

Her hand went to his belt buckle. She knew what she wanted.

"Paige."

His voice was hoarse and she reveled in the husky undertone. "Don't think, Jude. Just feel."

"But…"

"No worries." She pulled his shirt out of his jeans and her hands splayed across his roughened masculine skin. After that, there was no turning back for either of them. She unsnapped his shirt with lightning speed and her T-shirt was gone in an instant. The rest of their clothes were thrown to the floor.

And they were skin on skin, renewing all those feelings that had been dormant for way too long. He lay back and she lay on top of him, enjoying his hardened muscles, which fit perfectly into hers. His hands touched all those sensitive places he knew so well and she in turn stroked and caressed every inch of him until they both were sweaty, panting and beyond rational thought.

He rolled her onto her back and they came together in perfect harmony, as they always had. The moment his body joined hers, a thought ran through her head: *Welcome home.* That was the way it felt. She was home in his arms.

She bit into his shoulder as pleasure rocketed through her body. The taste of salt and blood filled her senses and she wanted to remember this moment forever. Because she knew beyond any doubt that their love would never end.

JUDE BREATHED DEEPLY and tried to calm his racing heart but he was far from calm. He was charged. Fulfilled. Complete. In a way that only she could make him feel.

He softly kissed her nose, her mouth, then trailed down to her tender breast. Her skin was a satiny palette and he soaked up every sweet nuance that was Paige. His Paige. His beautiful, intelligent, incredibly naive Paige.

The hum of a passing car outside invaded his fantasy. His paradise. He winced at the reality. He drew away and pulled her with him. They lay together in the darkened room as the outside world went on. For a moment in time the world had stood still. Just for them. Now he had to face one more mistake.

Loving her didn't feel like a mistake.

He'd forgotten her. Gotten over her. Now everything was as real and new as ever.

But it still was a mistake.

Her life wasn't in Horseshoe. His would always be. He pushed it to the never-never part of his mind and held her because he couldn't let go just yet. He selfishly held on to these minutes that he needed just to survive.

She slept peacefully in his arms. Content. Her breath fanned his cheek and a pain shot through him as he pulled away and reached for his clothes. Silently, he dressed. She slept on and he was grateful for that. He had to go. His son was waiting. Their son.

Unable to resist, he kissed her one more time.

"Jude," she murmured.

He took a long breath and walked out of the room. As he did, he was very aware that he'd made everything that much worse. How many mistakes could one man make in a lifetime?

PAIGE WOKE UP to a lethargic feeling. She rolled over and reached for Jude, and all her hand encountered was an empty spot. He'd gone. But then, she'd known that he would. Their son needed him. She was just happy that he'd come last night to help soothe her aching heart. She pulled the sheet over her naked body and went back to sleep.

Two hours later she was up and dressed and busy painting, but her thoughts were on Jude and Zane and she hoped her son was much better this morning. She kept waiting for a phone call from Jude to let her know how things were, but it never came. By midafternoon she knew it wouldn't. His quietness now would test her patience.

ZANE SLEPT UNTIL ten the next morning and at first it worried Jude. But his son had had a rough Saturday, so Jude let him sleep in, knowing he needed the rest. When he woke up, he was bubbly and chatty, as always. The ankle was a little more swollen and Zane said it didn't hurt that bad. Jude didn't give him any more medication, because he wanted to save it for when he really was in pain.

After a shower, Zane changed into shorts and a T-shirt. "Look at my trophy, Dad." He stood on one foot in front of the dresser where it was displayed, stroking it lovingly. He ignored the box his mother had given him, sitting next to it.

They were back to pretending Paige didn't exist. Zane hobbled around on one foot and Jude helped him down the stairs to the living room. His grandmother made a fuss over him and Zane was all smiles. Jude just hated that once again they would have to tackle the subject of the elephant in the room: his mother. But not until later.

"I'm making a special dinner just for you," his grandmother told him. "Chicken-fried steak, mashed potatoes and gravy."

"Oh, boy."

"It's almost eleven. Would you like a glass of milk or something to hold you over?"

"Okay."

"Dad, could you bring my trophy downstairs, please?"

Jude did as his son requested and the morning passed quickly as the whole family turned out to cheer up Zane. He was the center of attention, except when baby John stole it every now and then wanting to kiss Zane's boo-boo.

Over lunch, Zane talked about the race and Dudley hitting him with the crop. Jude was glad he was talking about it, because he didn't want him suppressing that, too.

"The next time I see Dudley McCray, I'm going to beat the crap out of him," Elias said.

Zane's face crumpled. "No, Uncle Elias, don't do that."

"Hey, buddy, I was just joking," his brother hastened to reassure him.

"Good, because I don't want you to hurt him. It doesn't feel good to be hurt."

Elias did something unexpected. He got up and hugged Zane. "No one's going to hurt you again."

There was gut-wrenching silence around the table and then Phoenix slayed the emotion-stealing moment with, "Who wants to play poker this afternoon?"

"I do!" Zane shouted, and Jude stared at his son. His brothers played poker a lot and Zane had never shown any interest in it.

"You got any money?" Elias asked with a gleam in his eye.

"Yes. It's in my room." Zane looked at Jude. "Can you get it, Dad?"

"I don't know if I want you playing poker with…"

"Dad, please."

"The boy wants to learn, so let him," was Grandpa's response. "I'll make sure these ya-hoos don't mistreat him."

Jude had never feared for one moment that his brothers would mistreat Zane. He was just hoping that he and Zane could have some time alone this afternoon. But maybe fun time with his uncles would be best.

He gave his son five dollars out of his pocket and told him when he lost that, the game was over. But he knew his son. He learned things quickly and easily. If his brothers and Grandpa didn't watch out, he'd clean their clocks.

Jude left his son in his brothers' hands and went to his saddle-making workshop to be alone. He had to think. Paige filled his mind so completely that he had to get his thoughts straight. He'd wanted to call her this morning but had thought better of that. He had to talk to her soon, though. He just wasn't sure what to say. Being quiet solved a lot of problems. He didn't have to stress over words. That left a big wad of emotions that were never expressed. And it was the reason he'd found himself at a hospital signing away his rights to his son. He never wanted to go back to being that person.

The moment he opened the door, the scent of leather greeted him and he relaxed. His parents had worried about the fact that he was so quiet, and they'd wanted to get him involved in something that would help him. So he'd taken woodworking and leather craft in school just to get them off his back. To his surprise, he'd loved it and he'd loved the teacher, who had taught him so much. He'd diligently worked at his craft and improved. It was something he was proud of and something he could talk about. Now it was more than a hobby. Every saddle he sold went into Zane's college fund. But Zane would very likely be like his mother and receive a full scholarship. There would be extras, though, and Jude wanted to be prepared. He spent many evenings cutting and working with leather.

A black saddle with silver conchas took pride of place in front of his desk. He'd made the saddle for his father when he was fifteen and his father had used it until the day he died. One day Jude would give it to Zane, who had never met his grandfather. Jude wanted his son to have a part of the man who had shaped Jude's life.

He picked up a soft cloth and leather cream

and rubbed it into the saddle. Every time he did this, he felt closer to his father. The leather was smooth and had a sheen to it. Jude leaned back on his desk and stared at the saddle. He could almost hear his father's words. *Do your best, son. That's all I'll ever ask of you.*

I'm trying, Dad, Jude replied silently. *I still love her, but I don't see a future for us.*

"Jude?"

Chapter Fourteen

"Paige." Jude swung around with a startled look on his face.

"I don't mean to intrude, but a guy with long hair and a scar on his face told me you were in here. I wanted to know how Zane is today. I thought you would call."

"I've been busy." His words were testy and the new feelings of the morning began to fade. "He's pretending you don't exist and I'm giving him time before I force it again."

She drew a steadying breath and looked around the room, with its tables covered with leather pieces, a working stool, different machines, a big sink, leather-making tools covering one wall and a big desk. "You have your own shop now."

"Yeah, I built it about two years after Zane was born. I needed to make extra money for him. I wanted him to have everything."

Her throat clogged at the accusing implication, and the man who'd made love to her last night was gone. A cold stranger was staring back at her. She walked over to the black saddle and touched it. "I remember when you made this in school. We weren't dating then, but everyone knew how excited you were to give it to your dad."

"Yeah. I never dreamed he would die that quickly."

"I'm so sorry about that. I know how much you loved him."

He stared at the rag in his hand. "I wish he could've seen Zane. He would have loved him." He moved to a table and placed the rag on it and then turned to her. "What are you doing here?"

"I wanted to check on Zane."

"I wished you'd called first."

"I did, but you didn't answer your phone."

He patted his shirt pockets and then his jeans. "I must've left it at the house."

"How's he feeling?"

"Sad, but my brothers are cheering him up."

"I see." She should have never come here, but with the newfound emotions of the night, she couldn't stay away. Clearly it was only one-sided. But she wasn't going to walk away without an explanation. "What's wrong? You're different this afternoon."

He swallowed visibly and remained silent, as he always did. That angered her. She had hoped he'd outgrown that.

"If you don't talk, we can't solve anything."

"You want me to talk? Okay." His words were sharp, as if he'd been honing them for years. "When you first came back, you said there was nothing here for you. And you said the same thing over twelve years ago. I'm here, Paige. Didn't that mean anything to you?"

"Of course it did."

"No, it didn't. You went on with your plans as if I didn't exist."

"That's not true. We talked about the baby and you never offered any solutions. I kept waiting, Jude, for you to make suggestions, but you never did. So don't lay a guilt trip on me."

He took a deep breath and stared at the ceiling. "When I took you to Austin to the airport, you kept crying, and I didn't know what to say to you. Words were just not there. When did we stop talking? That's what I'd like to know. When did we start forgetting the important stuff?"

"The moment I told you I was pregnant, things changed. You were different and more quiet than usual. That's why I listened to Mrs.

Carstairs. But we both decided the baby would be better off with a loving couple."

"We were a loving couple!" he shouted, and for a moment a spasm of fear gripped her. "I just kept thinking we were doing the right thing, but in my heart I knew we weren't. I focused on you and your career and your dreams and I should've been focusing on the baby and his life and his dreams."

She wanted him to talk and now she had to listen and she had to bear each word, even though they cut right through her skin.

"I was going to join Phoenix and Paxton and rodeo that summer. I had to pack and I was going to meet them in Amarillo the next day. But every mile I drove toward Horseshoe, I wasn't thinking about the rodeo. I was thinking about that baby I left behind. He was mine. He had my blood and the closer I got to Horseshoe, the more the rodeo faded from my mind. I couldn't live with myself if I just walked away. Telling my mother was the hardest thing I've ever had to do, besides giving my son away. She supported me and I was able to get Zane back and I will always be grateful for that. I've protected him for over twelve years now. Everything I do is for Zane."

He ran both hands through his hair and seemed to stagger with all the words that had come out of him. Words he'd never said before. "I knew nothing about babies. I'd bounced Eden around and played with her, but I never fed her or changed her diapers. It was a rude awakening for an eighteen-year-old boy. I learned everything I had to do, and for someone who slept soundly, I learned to wake up at the slightest noise because Zane might need me. It wasn't easy by any means and I've made so many bad decisions. But if Zane doesn't want to see you again, I'm going to ask you to leave."

"No, Jude, please." The plea came from deep

within her and she would beg if she had to. She might not deserve it, but she was willing to do anything to be a part of her son's life.

"How long do you plan to stay in Horseshoe?" he asked instead of answering.

The question flustered her. "I don't know. As long as it takes."

"But you have to go back?"

"Yes, I have to finish my residency."

"And what about Zane? You're going to walk away from him once again?"

"Why are you being so mean?"

"Because I'm a father and I have to look out for what's best for my son. If he gets to know you and you leave, how do you think he's going to feel?"

She hung her head and stared at the concrete floor as twelve years came full circle and she now had to face the biggest decision of her life. This time she would get it right, even if it meant giving up everything she'd ever worked for. But Jude wasn't going to believe that.

"I'm not trying to be mean," he said before she could formulate a response. "I thought about it since last night. I'm falling back into that old pattern of trying to comfort you and then we have sex and that doesn't solve anything. It only makes everything much worse. We have to stop now and put Zane first."

She gathered the remnants of her shattered pride and raised her head to stare into his dark troubled eyes. "I know you want me to leave, but I'm not going to. Zane knows I'm here and I'm hoping eventually he'll open the box and want to see me. That's my last hope and until it's gone, I'm not going anywhere." On feet that felt as heavy as lead, she walked to the door.

"Paige."

She turned to look at him one more time. "You can stop talking now, Jude. Really."

JUDE SAT IN his chair, leaned his head back and waited for the roof to cave in on him. That was the way he felt, as if his world had just been destroyed. But he'd done what was needed to protect Zane and to protect himself.

It was just as Phoenix had said: Jude had barely survived the first time and he couldn't do it again. As much as he loved her, there was no future for them. There hadn't been years ago and there wasn't now. God only knew why they were so attracted to each other.

With a sigh, he got up and went in search of his son. Zane was all that mattered to him. Laughter rode on the afternoon breeze and brightened the spring day. It was Zane. The death grip on his heart eased at the sound. His son was happy again.

He stopped as he saw Quincy, Jenny and Zane coming toward him. Quincy had Zane piggyback and was evidently taking him to the house.

"Hey, Dad," Zane shouted. "Uncle Quincy took me to see Bear and Little Dove."

"I see," he said as he reached them. "Is the poker game over?"

Zane slid to the ground and stood on one foot. "I made a bunch of money. Grandpa says he's not playing with me anymore. And Uncle Elias wants to know how I did it. I told him I just learned it."

Jude mussed his son's hair. "It's time for you to get some rest."

"Aw, Dad."

Jude squatted in front of the boy and Zane climbed onto his back. "Thanks for taking care of him," Jude said to Quincy and Jenny.

"No problem." Quincy waved as they walked away.

"Where did you go, Dad?" Zane asked.

To rip my heart out.

"I'm starting a new saddle and had to get some things done while you were busy."

"Oh."

"How's the foot?"

"Good. I haven't been walking on it."

As they made their way to the house, Zane laid his head against Jude's. That one little action showed Jude his son was still torn up inside. He wanted to be close to his father. Zane didn't have to worry. Jude was doing everything he could to protect him. But it came with a dose of regrets followed with a chaser of what-could-have-been.

PAIGE WENT HOME and painted and painted. If she kept busy, she couldn't think, and that was what she wanted. Just to be numb for a while to let the pain sink in so she could deal with it.

The green in her mother's bedroom didn't suit her, so she drove to Temple to buy more paint. She knew she wasn't acting rational, but that didn't matter, either. She was just going through the motions.

This time she bought candy-apple red and painted one wall. The rest she painted wheat. Even though she wasn't crazy about the color it accented the red. She stood back and looked at her handiwork. It was fiery, loud and bold. Just like her mother. It was perfect.

She had no idea what time it was. It was dark outside and her eyelids grew heavy. She curled up on the carpet to rest a bit. That was where Staci found her the next morning.

Staci sat on the floor beside her. "What's wrong? Are you high on all this paint? It smells in here."

"I have the windows opened."

"I've been calling and you're not answering your phone."

Paige stretched her shoulders. "I've been busy."

"Why are you sleeping on the floor?"

Paige brushed hair out of her eyes and realized her ponytail had come undone. A lot of things had come undone, and she pushed everything down inside her, not wanting to talk about it.

"Don't do that."

"What?"

"Pretend you're not upset. What happened?"

All kinds of lies ran through her head to tell her sister so she wouldn't worry, but she was too tired to voice any of them. What did it matter? Nothing seemed to matter anymore.

She got to her feet and went to the kitchen to make coffee. Staci followed. Sitting at the kitchen table, she bared her soul because she was too weak to do anything else.

"Zane was hurt yesterday and now Jude wants you to leave?"

She swallowed the sob in her throat. "Yes. Then we wouldn't have to face that we have a problem. Zane doesn't want to see me or have anything to do with me and Jude doesn't want to push him."

"Oh, honey, I'm sorry."

Staci got up and brought the coffee back to

the table. "He just needs time, Paige. Don't let it get to you."

"I'm like a pincushion and I don't think one more stick is going to bother me, but it just might do me in, too. I deserve all of this and that's what makes me so sad. What kind of mother would allow someone to persuade her to give her child away?"

"I'm not even going to answer that, because you're feeling sorry for yourself and that's not the way to handle this. I firmly believe that everything you did was for that baby's welfare. Since I lived with our mother, I know exactly how you were feeling, so no one had better ever say that to me."

A hint of a smile threatened her lips. "It's nice to have someone in my corner."

"I'm there, kiddo. Always." Staci played with her cup. "I'm not saying this to hurt you or anything, but you were always so sensitive about what Mom said to you. You always took it to heart. Whereas Luke and I let it wash right over us. We were good at running out the door to friends just to get away from her. But you always stayed so she wouldn't be alone. That was your first big mistake."

Paige stared at the new yellow paint on the wall, bright and sunny, and it reminded her of something. "When you graduated and packed your things to leave for your new job in Temple, I was sad because I felt more alone than ever. Mom went out and bought me a pretty yellow sundress and sandals to match. It was so beautiful. I went down to the bakery and hung out with Angie, Rachel and Jenny. I had nice clothes just like they did and I felt a part of the group. I came home later that evening and Mom was drunk in the front yard. She couldn't even make it to the door. I helped her get into the house and all my newfound confidence just evaporated. Funny how I remember that one little incident, and her kind gesture was then like a slap in the face, as so many other things were."

Staci clapped her hands loudly and Paige jumped. "I want you to stop this. Stop all the remembering. You don't see me doing that. I put it all behind me and so has Luke. Now you have to do the same."

Paige took a gulp of coffee. "Why can't I?"

Staci reached across the table and clasped Paige's hand. "Listen to me. Mom asked about you all the time and she told the people at the facility that her daughter was smart and becoming a doctor."

"She did?"

"Yes, one of the nurses even asked me if it was true and I told her it was. I think she treated you badly after Luke and I left because it was her way of forcing you to stay. If she criticized and demeaned you enough, you wouldn't have the confidence to do anything else but stay. She had a fear of being alone, so she did everything she could to keep you here. When you left, she fell apart. She stayed drunk all the time and I had so many calls to come do something with her and I finally did when she fell and broke her hip. I knew it was time. I think she just really missed you."

A tear slipped from Paige's eye and she remembered all the times she was there to help her mom and all the times she was so embarrassed and all the times she wished her mom was someone else. Life had a funny way of showing the past through a two-way mirror. Paige needed her mother and her mother needed Paige. But they'd never made the connection as mothers and daughters should. And that was the saddest thing of all.

She drew a deep breath and let it flow through her system and wash away all the inner turmoil that had been building in her. It was time to let it go. Her childhood had shaped her into an insecure, naive teenager. But she had grown stronger and she'd built a life of making decisions and choices that were better for her and now she had to embrace the present with all that confidence and go after what she wanted. She had to stop feeling sorry for herself. She had to stop blaming everyone else. She had to take full responsibility for her life.

No one was talking her into doing something she didn't want to do. Not ever again.

Not even Jude.

JUDE WAS UP early and showered. He slipped into jeans and quickly ran a razor over his face. He had to take Zane to the doctor, so looking presentable was required. Otherwise he wouldn't, because they would be baling hay today and it required no personal maintenance.

As he was snapping his shirt, he heard Zane moving around in his room and he went to see what his son was up to. The boy was stuffing books into his backpack.

"What are you doing? You're not going to school. You have to go to the doctor this morning."

Zane grabbed his jeans and sat on the bed to put them on. "I can go later. I have to go to school, Dad. I can't break my record. I haven't missed a day of school since second grade when I had the flu."

"The ER doctor said you had to rest for a couple of days. As soon as your doctor's office is open, I'm going to call and see if he can work you in. We'll take it from there."

"No." Zane zipped his jeans. "When Aunt Rachel comes, I'm getting in her car and going to school and you can't stop me."

Not one of those days, please.

Jude placed his hands on his hips. "You want to say that again?"

Zane shook his head. "It took all my courage to say it the first time."

Jude didn't smile at the admission. When

Zane talked back, Jude had to apply all of his parenting skills. "This is how it's going, son. As I said, I'll call the doctor's office as soon as it's open and you're going to go in. If he says you can go to school, then I'll take you. But if he says no, you're coming home and spending the day with Leah and baby John."

"Aw, Dad."

"Do you need some help getting dressed?"

"No."

"I'll help you downstairs when you're ready."

"You treat me like a baby."

Jude stared at his son. This was so unlike him and Jude knew it was because of everything that happened over the weekend. But Jude had rules for his son and he didn't want him to be a spoiled brat.

"And you're treating me with disrespect."

Zane's eyes opened wide. "I just want to go to school."

"You will when the doctor says you can. This

conversation is over, Zane, and you better get in a better frame of mind, because I'm losing my patience."

Jude headed to his room and finished dressing. When he went back into Zane's room, his son was dressed with the backpack in his hand. Jude noticed the trophy tucked inside, the top sticking out. He sighed, not wanting to get into another argument. He'd deal with the trophy later.

He piggybacked him downstairs to the kitchen. All the brothers were there and Zane perked up. As they ate breakfast, the doorbell rang. Jude pushed his plate back and went to see who it was.

The sheriff, Hardy Hollister, the DA, a woman who Jude thought was Malachi's wife and Dudley stood there.

Now what?

Chapter Fifteen

"Could we speak to you for a minute, Jude?" the sheriff asked.

Jude stepped aside and followed them into the den. After everyone was seated, Wyatt continued, "This is about what happened on Saturday."

Jude rested his forearms on his knees with his hands clasped together. "I figured as much. Dudley deliberately beat my son to win a race. I'm not happy about that."

"I'm not, either, Mr. Rebel," the woman said. "Actually, I'm quite horrified by the fact that my son would do this."

Jude looked at Wyatt, trying not to be swayed by the woman. "What do you want from me, Wyatt?"

"Mrs. McCray is asking for leniency, but I'm not inclined to be too lenient. If this had happened to my kid, I'd probably file charges."

"Then I don't understand what you're doing here. You're the law. Do what you have to."

"He'll be charged with assault and sent to juvie for time specified by the judge. He'll have a criminal record."

"I don't have a problem with that. Dudley has picked on Zane for years and it has to stop. That time is now."

"Please, Mr. Rebel," the woman pleaded. "I'm begging you. It's not Dudley's fault. He's influenced by his father, who routinely beats him. I'm finally standing up for my kids. From this day forward he'll never lay a hand on one of them again, nor will he lay a hand on me in anger. If you will give my child a second chance, I promise he'll never be mean to your son again. We'll pay all the hospital bills and whatever you want us to do."

Jude didn't let the desperation in the woman's voice get to him. "How can I be assured he won't hurt my kid again? Zane has scars that he will have for the rest of his life and showing mercy to a kid who did that is just not in my nature. And Malachi is an angry, bitter man. He will continue to do what he always does and I don't think your stand now is going to help."

"I already told Malachi that if he does anything to harm my children again, I will leave and take them with me and he'll never see them again. My family is a Christian family and I'd never been hit in my whole life until I married Malachi. I'm tired, Mr. Rebel, of this kind of lifestyle, but it was my choice and now I'm trying to make it work for my kids. But if it doesn't, I will be gone and you have my word on that."

"Ma'am—"

"My name is Cheryl," she interrupted.

He didn't want to know her name or anything else about the McCray family. He clenched his jaw, refusing to make this personal. "Ma'am, Dudley hurt my kid badly and I just can't overlook that."

"Dad." Zane hopped into the room and held on to the sofa. Jude got to his feet. He didn't want Zane to hear this. "Don't do it."

"Zane, go back to the kitchen."

"I was the one who was hurt and I should have a say in Dudley's punishment."

Dudley sat with his head bowed and hadn't moved or spoken a word and Jude had to wonder if this was all his mother's doing. He looked at the boy. "What do you have to say, Dudley?"

"Send me to jail. I don't care."

His mother paled and put her arm around

him. "Lose the attitude and tell these people how you really feel. Tell them how you cried at what you'd done and you asked me a dozen times to call and see how Zane was doing. You didn't mean to hurt him."

"I didn't," Dudley muttered. "But I was afraid I was going to get beaten again and I had to win and I didn't know what else to do." The boy raised his head and turned to look at Zane. "I'm sorry I hurt you. But you're so smart and you're always so perfect it makes me mad."

"Is that why you call me names?" Zane asked.

"I guess."

"Do you promise to never call me names again and to never be mean to me again?"

Dudley nodded with a glimmer of hope in his eyes. "Yes."

Zane looked at his father. "I don't want to press charges, Dad."

"I'm not just letting this drop, son."

"It's not going to be dropped, Jude," Hardy said, getting to his feet. "If you agree, I'll ask the judge for a probation period for three months. During that time if Dudley does one thing to harm Zane or anyone else, he'll serve some time in juvie."

"But he has to keep his nose clean and Malachi has to abide by the rules, too," Wyatt said. "I'll make sure he understands them. And Mrs. McCray will see to everything else. Is that okay with you?"

Hell, no!.

But he looked at his son and saw forgiveness as bright as the sun shining outside. Zane had a big heart and Jude had to wonder why that consideration wasn't extended to his mother.

"Yes, and my son will be well watched by everyone in this family."

"I understand." The sheriff nodded and the group walked toward the door.

"Thank you, Mr. Rebel." The woman offered her hand and he shook it.

"Considering the relationship between the Rebels and McCrays, I told Mrs. McCray this was a waste of time," Wyatt added, standing at the door. "Maybe the younger generation is getting it right. Thanks, Jude." They shook hands.

Jude returned to his son. "That was very understanding of you."

"Dudley comes to school a lot with bruises on his arms and face and that has to be rough, to be beaten all the time."

"But he hurt you."

"I know." Zane looked down at the sofa. "But I don't want to hurt him. I would like it if we could just live in peace."

He'd never been more proud of his son than he was at that moment. Jude was still leery about the McCrays, though. But he was willing to offer the olive branch in hopes that peace was a viable thing for everyone.

His brothers had a lot to say about the olive branch, but Jude ignored them and called the doctor for Zane. The nurse said they could work him in at 8:30 a.m. if Jude could get him there. They were on the road to Temple in five minutes.

The doctor said everything was healing nicely and didn't see any reason for Zane not to go to school, except for the ankle. He'd received the X-rays on his computer from the ER, and as the ER doctor had said, there were no broken bones or sprains. It was merely bruised and would need a few days to heal. He suggested crutches and Jude bought them at the pharmacy nearby. The pharmacist showed Zane how to use them and Jude had Zane back in Horseshoe and at school by ten o'clock.

Zane grabbed his backpack from the backseat and Jude noticed the trophy sticking out and once again he thought he should say something. But Zane broached the topic first.

"Dad, would it be bragging if I showed off my trophy?"

"Yes, I think so, especially around Dudley and the McCrays. Why don't you take a couple of pictures and you can show Erin and Jody and all your girl friends."

"Dad." Zane sighed in irritation. "I have guy friends, too."

"I didn't notice that many on Saturday."

Zane removed the trophy from the backpack, took several pictures and then laid it on the backseat. "I'm a chick magnet. Maybe I take after Uncle Elias or Uncle Paxton." Zane laughed as he slipped on his backpack. He then hobbled toward the entrance to the school.

Jude waited until his son was in class before he went to see the principal to let him know what had happened and that he wanted Zane watched by all the teachers. The principal said he would take care of it. On his way out, he met Annabel in the hall.

"Jude, how nice to see you. How is Zane?"

He told her everything that had happened and added, "I'd appreciate it if you'd look out for him."

"No problem." She looked squarely at him. "How's it going with Zane's mother? I saw her and she really was amazing, the way she took care of his injuries."

"Yeah, she's an accomplished doctor, but things aren't going all that well. Zane refuses to see her and we're kind of in a holding pattern right now."

"I'm sure it will all work out." Her tone was different than it had been before. Cool and professional. Not like the extra-friendly teacher she had been.

"Thank you."

She walked off down the hall and Jude knew whatever they'd had was over. No one affected him like Paige. He might as well admit that. Also, he wasn't sure anything would've happened with Annabel even if Paige hadn't come back. Something was always holding him back. Or someone.

As he drove away from the school, he wanted to tell Paige how her son was doing. He wasn't apologizing for yesterday. He had to take a stand, even if it hurt. But he so badly wanted her to know that Zane was okay and back in school.

At the stop sign, he pulled out his phone to text her. His thumbs paused over the keypad. He couldn't keep doing this. He had to maintain some distance and texting her wasn't going to help their situation. He slipped the phone back into his pocket.

AFTER SHOWERING AND changing clothes, Paige was in a better state of mind. Seeing and talking to Staci was what she'd needed to get her head straight. After Staci left, she drove to the antiques store and bought a nightstand, a lamp and a picture frame.

She put Zane's photo in the frame and placed it by her bed. Again, she was just going through the motions. She had no plans to live in the house, only to keep busy, and she wanted her son's photo beside her.

The house had so many memories, but they weren't dragging her down like before. With the new paint, everything was fresh and bright, which was the way she wanted to feel inside. She would get there. It would just take time. She went to her mother's room and sat on the carpet cross-legged, staring at the red wall. All the yelling, screaming, crying, drunken binges, different men trailing in and out of their house, and people talking behind their backs cumulated into a hard ball in her stomach.

She sucked air into her lungs and she saw

her mother for who she was: a needy person, a person who desperately needed to feel loved. And she'd gotten that love the only way she'd known how. It had hurt her children, but her mother had never seen that. Paige sucked another breath into her chest and released it. She had to let go of all the bitterness and resentment. It was over and she couldn't keep reliving the moments that tainted her life, her future.

Drawing another breath, she whispered, "I forgive you." The ball in her stomach rose up, and instead of giving in to the nausea, she swallowed hard and let go. The ball dissipated and she felt relief for the first time in years. And just like the room, everything was fresh and new again.

She sensed she wasn't alone and she didn't need to turn to see who it was. His presence was undeniable. Jude.

Without taking her eyes off the wall, she said, "Did you get your second wind?"

"You asked me to talk and I did. I'm not apologizing for that. Zane is always my top priority."

She scooted to face him and then wished she hadn't. He leaned against the doorjamb in tight jeans and a blue shirt. His dark hair fell forward over his forehead as if he'd just removed his hat. Raw masculinity seemed to reach out and touch her and she desperately wanted to jump up and wrap her arms around him, to just feel his heart beating against hers. But she couldn't do that. As he'd said, Zane was now *their* top priority.

"What are you doing here?"

"I took Zane to the doctor this morning and he said everything was healing nicely. He just needs to rest his ankle for a few days. The doctor suggested crutches. I took him to school because he insisted and the doctor okayed it."

"I'm glad." She rubbed a paint spot on her jeans. "Did he open the box?" She didn't want to ask, but she couldn't help herself.

"No, it's sitting on his dresser. I don't think he's even glanced at it."

She bit her lip to keep the revelation from getting to her.

"I thought you'd like to know that he doesn't want me to file charges against Dudley McCray."

"Why? He viciously beat Zane."

"The sheriff and the DA came out to the house to talk to us. Dudley has his own problems with his father, and Zane doesn't want him to get into any more trouble than he's already in. Dudley is on probation. If he screws up, he's going to juvenile hall."

"That was very understanding and compassionate of Zane."

"Yeah. That's how he is. He's upset now because you've come back, but give him time."

Her heart felt heavy from the warmth cradling it. The fact that Jude had come over here to tell her that made all the difference in the world. There was no one like Jude. And her son was just like him.

"Thank you."

He pushed away from the doorjamb and said, "It's red."

"What?" She had no idea what he was talking about.

He nodded toward the wall. "You were staring at it as if you didn't know what color it was. It's red. Bright red."

She smiled. An honest-to-God smile that reached inside her and would buffet her emotions for days to come. "Uh…yeah. It's red."

Before the pregnancy had rocked their world, Jude used to tease her all the time, trying to cheer her up. He had a dry wit that always brought her out of the dumps and she was reminded of that today.

Without another word, he walked out of the room and out of the house. That was okay. That was pure Jude and she understood him better than anyone.

She got to her feet, feeling more optimistic than she had in a long time. Whatever the future held, she was ready to face it. With a man like Jude waiting on the sidelines, there was nothing else she could do. Or wanted to do.

IN THE AFTERNOON she decided to tackle the washer and dryer in the garage to see if they worked. She managed to pull the washer out and saw the hoses were cracked. A box of Luke's tools was in the garage. She removed the hoses and took them down to the hardware store to see if she could get new ones.

Bubba Wiznowski, Angie's brother, was in the store and he helped her to find what she needed and then came to the house and put them on. In no time, he had the washer working. And to her amazement, with a little cleaning, the dryer came on, too. Her first load of clothes was in the rinse cycle when she heard the doorbell.

She ran to the door in hopes it was Jude again. It wasn't. Rachel stood there.

"I don't mean to bother you."

"Come in. You're not bothering me."

"I don't have time. I'm on my way home. Since Zane is on crutches, Jude picked him up and I thought I'd stop by for a minute. Once a month we have a ladies' night out at Angie's office. We eat, drink, talk, laugh and have a good time. I was hoping you would join us. We'd love to have you come."

"Thank you, Rachel, for thinking of me, but under the circumstances, I don't think so."

Rachel rested her hand on the top of her stomach. "Just think about it. We get there around seven."

"Maybe next time. Thank you for being so nice."

"If you change your mind, we'll be there." Rachel turned away and Paige thought of something.

"Oh, Rachel. Does Mrs. Brimhall still teach at the school?"

"Yes, she's still teaching and a stickler for perfect English."

"Thank you. I might stop in to see her."

Paige waved to her friend as she drove away. It was nice of Rachel to ask, but she wasn't ready to face the people of Horseshoe. She had to see someone else first to exorcise the ghost from her past.

It was a little after four and she quickly drove to the school, feeling Mrs. Brimhall would still be there. Paige was in luck. A thin woman with salt-and-pepper hair sat behind a desk in Paige's old English classroom.

"Mrs. Brimhall."

The woman looked up and pushed her thick wire-rimmed glasses up the bridge of her nose. "Yes, dear. Can it wait until tomorrow? I was just closing up for the day."

"You don't recognize me, do you?" Paige walked farther into the room, and at the puzzled look on the woman's face, she added, "I'm Paige Wheeler."

"Oh, dear, how nice to see you. Should I call you Doctor now?"

"You can just call me Paige." She didn't want to go into detail. She just wanted answers. "I was looking for Mrs. Carstairs. I would like to see her while I'm in town."

"She moved away years ago."

Paige already knew that. "Do you have any idea where she lives?" Mrs. Brimhall and Mrs. Carstairs were close friends back then and Paige was hoping she would know where the woman lived now.

"Poor Nancy. She's had a rough time."

"What do you mean?"

"She and her husband so desperately wanted a child and they had an adoption all set up, but it fell through. Nancy never talked much about it, so I don't know what really happened, but afterward she and her husband divorced and Nancy moved to Austin to be closer to her sister. We stayed in touch for a while, but then she met Fred and he is really controlling. I haven't heard from her in years."

"So she remarried?"

"Yes." Mrs. Brimhall's forehead crinkled. "His name was Fred Wilhelm. Like I said, a grouchy, controlling man. I didn't like him, but Nancy was pleased about the marriage. He had three kids and she was happy to be their mother."

"I was so hoping to get to see her."

"Sorry. She lives in Austin now."

"Thank you, Mrs. Brimhall." She looked around the room at the desks, a chalkboard and the computers. "Everything looks the same, except for the computers."

"Oh, yeah. The world is changing, and I must say, I'm so happy that Horseshoe has a success story."

Paige left while she could. She had the information she wanted and now she would see Nancy Carstairs face-to-face. She couldn't even begin to heal until she saw the woman who had tried to steal her baby.

Chapter Sixteen

Paige was in Austin by seven that evening. She would have made it sooner, but the traffic was heavy. A gas station was on the right, so she pulled off the freeway to fill up. Afterward she sat in her car and did some checking on her phone to locate Nancy. It didn't take her long to find the address of Fred Wilhelm.

The house was in a nice subdivision in south Austin. She parked at the curb and checked out the redbrick home with a manicured lawn. Blooming flowers decorated the flower beds and hanging baskets hung on the porch. The suburban lifestyle. The good life.

Nancy had certainly moved on and Paige took a moment to question what she was doing here. It wasn't going to change a thing, but something in her needed to see the woman who'd led her down a path to total devastation. Before she could go forward, she had to deal with all her feelings about Nancy Carstairs.

Getting out of the car, she took a deep breath and marched up the brick walk to the front door. She rang the doorbell and waited. The door opened and Nancy stood there looking much the same as she had almost thirteen years ago. Her blond hair was now streaked with gray and she'd gained some weight, but she still was the woman Paige had trusted with her life.

"Can I help…? Oh…Paige!"

Paige walked past her into the foyer before Nancy could shut the door in her face. "Yes, it's me. I bet you thought you would never see me again."

"Please leave." Nancy's voice was shaky. "I have nothing to say to you."

"That's too bad, because I have a lot to say to you. I trusted you and I trusted that you were giving me good advice, but instead you were devious and underhanded and did everything you could to make sure I gave my baby away."

"The baby was a burden to you and I offered you a good solution to go off to college and have your dream."

"As a naive teenage girl, I believed every word you said. I was conflicted and torn, but I wanted my baby to have the very best of everything. And you told me many times that my home environment was not a place to bring a baby into. You also told me that it would be detrimental for me to hold the baby or to even know the sex. All of that was bull. You see, I'm in obstetrics now and we stress to teenage girls that it is very important to hold their baby and to say goodbye. If they can do that, then they can deal with the aftermath of giving the child away."

"What do you want from me?"

"Nothing. My mother passed away and I came home from the funeral to learn that my son was being raised by his father. It was a shock at first, but now it's an incredible gift that I will always be grateful for. And I will forever be grateful that Jude chose that moment to stand up and speak up for our child."

Nancy twisted her hands nervously. "I would've given that baby a good home."

"He has a good home, the very best, with his biological family."

"Why did you come here? Yes, I deceived you, but it was for a good reason. Your baby would've been well taken care of and I would've loved it. I didn't feel I was doing anything wrong."

Paige stepped closer to her. "It's wrong to deceive a teenage girl so you can have her child.

I'm sure it's illegal, too, but that's all over with. I just have this need to see your face so that I can put it all behind me."

"Nancy," a male voice called, and in a few seconds a man entered the room with three young children behind him. "We're waiting for dessert." The man looked at her with a deep frown. "Who is this?"

"It's a student from Horseshoe. She stopped by to say hi."

"It would have been nice if she had called. This is our dinnertime."

Paige faced the man with the accusing voice. "Yes, it would be nice if people were considerate." She turned and walked to the door and Nancy followed her. At the door, she said, "I was going to tell you that I hoped you rot in hell, but I think you're already there."

She drove away with a feeling of elation, as if she'd slayed the dragon and victory was hers.

But victory was short-lived. She had a long way to go to banish all the ghosts from her past.

WHEN JUDE DROVE up to the house with Zane, Phoenix was just rolling up on a Polaris Ranger. "Hey, Zane, this is what you can use to get around on until your ankle heals."

"Why didn't I think of that?" Zane hobbled to the ATV and climbed on. He revved it up. "I'm going to check on Bear." And off he went to the barn. Jude and Phoenix followed.

"How's he doing?" Phoenix asked.

"Trying to forget that his mother exists."

"That can't be good for him. He doesn't have to love her or anything, but in my opinion, it would be good for him to talk to her without all the anger. A lot of mistakes were made back then, but now's the time to make it right again."

"Yeah, but I'm going to give it time. I just

don't know how long Paige is going to stay here, though. She never answered me."

Phoenix stopped walking and stared at Jude. "Then ask again. Speak up, for heaven sakes, Jude. Don't let her get away with evasive tactics. Zane is involved, too, now. You know you're never going to love anybody but Paige. Everybody knows that. No one in Horseshoe has ever asked about Zane's mother, because they know. They just don't know how it happened. And no one is brave enough to ask that to your face. It's time to bring all this out into the open and figure out your life with Paige or without her."

Jude stared off to the evening sun sinking in the west. Phoenix was right. He had to figure out what was best for all of them. But first Zane had to understand why his mother had done what she'd done, and he didn't know how long that would take.

He'd told himself that morning that he

wouldn't stop by and see Paige. But he'd found himself at the little house all the same. He'd known she was hurting and he was the cause of some of that hurt. That bothered him because he didn't like hurting people. And then she was staring at that damn wall and he couldn't figure out why. Of course, he hadn't asked. At that point, he'd rather not have known—he was sure it had something to do with her mother. Her whole life revolved around a mother who'd never loved her or cared about her and he sincerely hoped she was finding peace with that.

Later, Zane was tired. Walking on crutches took a lot of extra energy. After supper and a shower, Zane was out for the night. And the box was left unopened on the dresser.

The days fell into a pattern and Zane never mentioned his mother or the box. By Friday the swelling in his ankle had gone down and Zane said it didn't hurt to step on it. The crutches found a home in the closet. Since Zane was doing so well, Jude was wondering whether to force the issue once again. Paige had texted every day to ask about Zane and it was a real test of his patience not to go over and talk to her. She'd been back only a week and he realized how much he missed seeing her, talking to her, touching her. Oh, man, he was in so much trouble.

PAIGE SPENT HER days working on the house and in the yard as she waited. She pulled weeds out of the flower beds and planted new flowers. She made a trip down to the antiques store and bought things for the house. That was a little insane since she wasn't planning on staying there, but it kept her busy. She walked around the town and spoke to people and renewed her love of the small town. But she grew doubtful that her son was ever going to acknowledge her.

Jude stayed away, and every time she heard

a car, she'd run to the window to see if it was him. Sadly, it never was and she began to see just how much she needed him. How much she needed to simply hear his voice and be with him. They'd been apart too long. Was there still a chance for them?

ON SATURDAY, JUDE, Elias and Jericho worked on the hay baler. They usually hired a man to bale the hay, but since he'd raised his prices, Falcon had decided it would be cost effective if they took up the task themselves again.

After lunch on Sunday, Jude worked in his saddle shop and Zane played poker with Grandpa and the brothers. But Jude's mind was totally on Paige and how she was handling the wait. Tonight he might broach the subject with Zane. He was in a better mood and might listen. Jude had to make his son understand his world wasn't going to change if he spoke to his mother. It was just something he needed to do for his own peace of mind.

A thought kept running through his mind: Once Paige visited with her son, would she be gone from their lives again? That cut deep into Jude. Would she stay or would she go? And would he survive this time?

When he went back to the house, his mother was alone in the den. "Where's Zane?"

"He went upstairs a long time ago. I hope he's feeling okay."

"I'm sure he is. He's probably counting the money he won at poker."

"They had a lot of fun. It's good to see him happy again." His mom closed the farm and ranch magazine she was reading. "I try to stay out of my sons' childrearing decisions, but…"

"I'm on it, Mom. I'm just waiting for the right moment." He took the stairs two at a time to avoid a discussion on what he should or shouldn't do. He didn't need any advice, not even from his mother.

Jude went through his room into the bathroom, washed his hands and then continued into Zane's room. He stopped short in the doorway. Zane was in the middle of his bed with children's books all around him. Paige's box sat at the foot of the bed, opened.

Children's books? The box had been filled with children's books?

"Dad, listen."

Jude pushed the box aside to do just that.

Zane read from one of the books. "'My precious baby, today I felt you move for the first time and realized that a tiny human being is growing in me. Someone your dad and I created. A gift from God. That fills me with so much joy. I want to make all the right decisions for you because I want you to grow up to be a strong, healthy and secure person.'" He held the book out to Jude. "See, my mother wrote messages to me in all of the books. Want to hear another one?"

"Sure." Paige had never told him about the books, but then, they hadn't talked much about the baby, just what they needed to do. Avoidance was their mode of communication back then.

"'My precious baby, I'm sitting in the bathtub reading to you because you fill my every waking thought. My mother is yelling at me and I'm trying to shut out her voice. I feel resentment and bitterness toward her. I can't bring a precious baby into the house, because I feel she will poison you like she's poisoned me. I want the very best life for you and I'm afraid that means I will have to let you go. It will break my heart, but I want you to have everything that I never had. I want you to have love.'"

Jude swallowed hard as all those old emotions churned inside him. He tried to concentrate on Zane and his reaction. That was what was important. Zane's eyes were bright and shining as if he'd just discovered something beautiful that only he understood.

"Here's another, Dad." Zane picked up a book and began to read. "'My precious baby, today your father and I will travel to Austin to bring you into the world. And today we will let go and it will be the hardest thing we'll ever have to do. But I believe in my heart we're doing the right thing for you. You'll have two loving parents who will treasure you and love you and give you all the things that you'll need in this world. I will think of you always. I love you, my precious baby.'"

There was silence for a moment and Jude was glad because words clogged his throat in a way that prevented him from speaking. He'd been right there with her through all of it, but he'd never felt it so deeply as he did at that moment as he experienced her pain, her suffering in letting go.

"There's a lot more about the counselor she spoke to who gave her advice and how she encouraged her to do the right thing for her baby. I don't like those, but I'm glad they're there because I can read what she was feeling at the time."

"*Brown Bear, Brown Bear* is my favorite. It's where she wrote she felt me move for the first time."

Jude swallowed the sob in his throat. "Do you want to talk about your mother?"

"She's pretty, isn't she?"

"Yes. I always thought so."

"She wrote in one of the books she over-ate because she was nervous and people never knew she was pregnant."

"That's true. Her mother's cruel behavior was hard on Paige and the reason she made so many bad decisions."

"She's a doctor now."

"Yes, she is. She's has a few more months

before she takes the Medical Licensing Exam and then she'll be working in obstetrics. Her favorite part is working with teenage girls who are undecided about adoption."

"Really?"

"Yes. She doesn't want another girl to go through what she did and she certainly doesn't want a girl listening to a counselor who does not have her best interest at heart."

There was silence again as Zane ran his fingers over the words inscribed inside a book, as if to soak up the message. "Dad, why did you never ask my mother to marry you?"

That was a tough question and he didn't want to lie to his son, but the explanation hung in his throat.

As if sensing Jude's difficulty, Zane said, "Were you afraid she'd say no?"

He looked into those dark eyes so much like his own and wondered if the kid was a mind reader. That was exactly how Jude had felt. If he had asked and she had said no, he would've been devastated. Fear was a powerful thing and he'd controlled his emotions until the moment he realized he'd lost his son. Losing Paige was something he still hadn't grown accustomed to.

"Yeah. Her life was set and if I had asked her to stay, she would have had to give it all up and I didn't have the courage to do that."

"You're the bravest person I know, Dad. How many teenage guys would go back and get their kid after he had been given up for adoption?" Zane flipped through the book without looking at Jude. "Do you ever regret doing that?"

"Not for a second." That answer was easy. That one action in his life would stand out until the day he died and probably beyond. It had taken every ounce of courage he had.

"I don't think I want to be a teenager. They're crazy. Even Eden was crazy. What happens to them?"

Jude smiled at his son. "You're a smart kid and I'm betting you can figure it out."

"Yeah. It's about girls and sex and all that stuff."

"Yes, and all that stuff."

Zane picked up a book and placed it back into the box. "Dad, do you think we can visit my mother?"

And just like that, the world had righted itself and his son was now ready to face the woman who'd given him life. Jude couldn't have been happier.

STACI CALLED, AND Paige went to Austin to spend some time with her. There was a big wedding reception at two and she wanted Paige to see all the decorations. She had never seen her sister's work, so she drove in to have lunch and see the spectacular wedding Staci was raving about.

Paige, who had never been one to flip through

wedding magazines, was impressed with the gala affair. The ballroom was decorated in pink and white and silver. She'd never seen so many flowers adorning tables, and just about everywhere, huge arrangements stood. Silver candelabras sat on the bride and groom's table, as did fine china, silver and crystal. Every chair was covered in white with a big pink bow on the back. Small pink boxes tied with white ribbon waited at each place setting.

"What's in the boxes?" she asked her sister.

Staci winked. "Chocolates, my dear."

"Everything's gorgeous." Paige looked around the room at all the beautiful decorations and wondered if tonight a young woman's fantasy would come true. She would marry her Prince Charming. Ah, how unrealistic that sounded. But it was every little girl's dream. Paige had found her prince and she had a sinking feeling he was never going to forgive her. But she would keep hoping and dreaming and maybe she wouldn't need all these decorations, just a four-leaf clover. And a prayer.

Things began to get a little hectic as Staci had to deal with the kitchen crew, the waitstaff, the decorators and the wedding planner. Paige kissed her sister goodbye and headed back to Horseshoe. She didn't want to be gone too long. She made it home at about four and took off her dress and heels and wondered what she was going to do for the rest of the evening.

Slipping on her jeans and a T-shirt, she thought she might walk around the town square and try to enjoy the evening. She might even stop in at the bakery and buy something delicious. A buzz interrupted her thoughts and she realized it was her phone in her purse in the kitchen.

She ran and fished it out and saw that it was Jude. He was calling, not texting. Could that mean…?

"Are you busy?" he asked.

344 Texas Rebels: Jude

"No. I went to Austin to see Staci and I just got back. Is Zane okay?"

"Yes. He's fine and walking without his crutches, as I told you."

"Oh, good. I thought something had happened."

"Something has. Could we come over for a minute?"

We. "Jude, do you mean you and Zane?"

"Yes."

Her heart raced and she had trouble pushing words from her throat. "Yes, I'll be waiting. Thank you."

She clicked off and ran around the house like a madwoman. Maybe she should put her dress and heels back on. No. Maybe she should put on some makeup. No. She already had makeup on. She ran her hands up her arms and felt cold and hot all at the same time. Her son was coming. Her son was coming. Her precious baby. She sank to the floor and began to cry. Uncontrollable sobs shook her body. It seemed as though she'd waited forever for this moment and she was so nervous she wanted to scratch her skin until it bled. But she'd outgrown that habit. She'd outgrown a lot of things.

The sobs subsided and she wiped tears away with her back of her hand. Rising to her feet, she drew a calming breath and went to the bathroom to wash her face. She had to get control of herself and she didn't have much time. Looking in the mirror, she saw she'd smeared her mascara. Oh, crap. She scrubbed her face clean and then applied lipstick. That was the best she could do.

She took several more calming breaths and forced herself to walk to the kitchen. Her son was coming, but she had no idea what he wanted to say. She had to brace herself for that. She had to brace herself for the reality that this was not going to go as she wanted. But it was a start. And she hoped her son had at least lost some of his anger.

The doorbell rang and she jumped.

Her precious baby was here.

Chapter Seventeen

With a shaky hand, Paige opened the door. Zane stood in front of his father with the box in his hands, his eyes bright but cautious. The resentment she'd witnessed last Saturday wasn't there anymore. A sense of relief washed over her.

"I read what you wrote in the books," Zane said. "Could you read them to me?"

"I'd like nothing better. Come in." She opened the door wider and they came into the house. Paige's knees were trembling and she had to calm down or she wasn't going to get through this. "There's not much furniture here, though we have a table and chairs in the kitchen."

Zane placed the box on the table and sat in a chair.

"Zane, I'm going over to ask Bubba some questions about the hay baler we're working on. I'll be back in half an hour."

"Okay, Dad."

Paige didn't want Jude to feel he had to leave—or maybe she just wanted someone else here as she faced her twelve-year-old son. Before she could voice her concerns, Jude was gone and she was left staring into the most beautiful eyes she'd ever seen, just like his father's.

"I read what you wrote in the books," Zane said again. "And it made me...I don't know... sad."

She pulled a chair close to him. "Why did it make you sad?"

"Because I thought you gave me away because you didn't want me."

Her breath caught at his admission.

"But as I read, I could see how much you
wanted me and how much you suffered in
making your decision. I really don't like the
counselor or your mother, but I don't know
them and I'm glad that I don't."

"It was a very difficult time, but I felt in my
heart I was doing the right thing for you. But
once I reached California, I knew I had made
the wrong decision and there was just no way
to turn back the clock."

"My dad said you lost your scholarship and
had to live in a homeless shelter."

"Yes, but I found there are good people out
there. People who helped me to find myself
again. And once I was on my feet, I worked
hard to accomplish a dream I'd had since I was
a girl, even though it cost me my baby."

"But it didn't. My dad came and got me. My dad, he's special."

"Yes, your dad is very special."

"He can do all sorts of things with horses and cows and he makes saddles and repairs hay balers and tractors. He can do just about anything, but he doesn't talk much. Grandma says he's been that way since Ezra McCray shot him."

"Sometimes people with as much character as your father don't need to say a word. People know how he feels." As she said the words, she knew they were true. Jude didn't need to talk to her. She knew how he felt.

After that, Zane had loads of questions and she answered each one as honestly as she could. Her son was a talker, so unlike his father. His eyes lit up as if there were candles burning behind them. It was a joy just to watch this amazing child who was hers. And Jude's.

She didn't say she was sorry and she didn't

ask for forgiveness. She didn't need to. It was clear her son had forgiven her. That was a miracle in itself.

All too soon Jude returned and she wanted to hold on to the moment and to never let it go. And to never let her son go again. But summoning the maturity she'd learned over the years, she hugged her son with everything that was in her heart and he hugged her back. It was a moment she would remember forever.

She saw her son every day after that. He continued to ask questions and she continued to answer them. She wanted him to know everything that had happened and some of the answers made her look bad. But she didn't care. She wanted to be honest with her son.

Jude was busy baling hay and he asked if she could pick up Zane from school. She happily agreed. Zane wanted her to meet his teachers. He had no qualms about telling people she was his mother. Every teacher she talked to told her how bright Zane was and how he was a pleasure to teach.

They went to the bakery to get kolaches and a drink and Zane told Angie's mom and everyone in the place that Paige was his mother. No one seemed surprised, not even Angie. They walked around the town square and Zane talked constantly, telling her about Horseshoe and its businesses as if she'd never been there. She listened avidly. They met Wyatt and Hardy on the courthouse lawn and once again Zane introduced her as his mother. And again they didn't seem surprised.

One afternoon Staci came to meet her nephew and there was no awkwardness at all as Zane chattered as if he'd known Staci all his life. Of course, most of his conversation was about his dad and it was very clear how much he loved Jude.

Everything was perfect, better than she'd ever imagined, except Jude wasn't there. He stayed away and she didn't know if that was on purpose or if he was busy. Or maybe he was just giving her time with their son. In a way, it hurt. She wanted to see him and share this experience with him.

JUDE WAS DOG tired from a full day of hauling hay. One more day and they would be through with the hauling. Then they would start on another pasture. It was a never-ending cycle during the summer.

He showered and changed clothes. Zane still wasn't home and Jude decided to go to his shop to work on a saddle. He should have just sat in a chair and rested, but when he did that, thoughts attacked him from all sides and he hated how his mind was filled with questions he couldn't answer. Hard work solved that problem. If he kept working, he'd be too tired to even think.

His mom stopped him before he could get

out the door. "Eat something before you go, and don't say no. You've been working all day and you need nourishment."

For the first time he realized he was hungry. He filled his plate with pot roast, vegetables and a hot roll and took it to the table to eat. His mother brought him a glass of tea.

"When is Zane coming home?"

"I told him he has to be home by seven. Although Paige helps him with his homework now, so I guess just any time will do, but he'll be home by seven."

"He hasn't eaten supper here all week and I miss him."

Me, too. But he didn't say that to his mom. He didn't want her to know he was concerned about the future.

"He's getting to know his mom and I want that to happen. I'm stepping back so it can."

His mom patted his shoulder. "You were always too nice for your own good."

Before Jude could find a response, Quincy came in. "I thought Zane would be here. I haven't seen my partner all week."

"He's with his mom," Jude said.

"Do you want something to eat?" his mom asked Quincy.

"No, Mom, thanks. Jenny will be home soon." He took a chair across from Jude. "How do you feel about all this?"

Jude took a big swallow of tea and pushed his plate away. "I just told Mom that I want Zane to get to know his mother. Now I'm going to work on a saddle for a while." He was out the door before they could say another word. He wasn't answering any more questions. It was his life and this time he wasn't asking anyone for advice. He was going solo.

He turned on the lights in the shop and sat in his chair, the scent of leather filling his senses. He'd started the tree, which was the seat of the saddle, and also cut the leather for the saddle horn. All he had to do was shape it and glue it to the tree. But he had no desire to get started. His thoughts were on his son. And Paige.

The past week he had felt left out. Paige never asked him to come when he got off work. She never asked him to do anything with them. And he understood that. But he couldn't deny that feeling of loneliness that was taking root in his soul again. Soon they had to talk and he dreaded that. It was his least favorite thing.

The door opened and Zane burst in. "Hey, Dad."

"Hey." His whole world lit up at the sight of his son. "Did you have a good day?"

"Yeah. Why are you still working?" His son answered too quickly and he didn't look at Jude.

"Because I have a saddle to finish."

Zane looked at the tree and then at him. "But you haven't done anything. It was like that days ago."

Jude stretched his shoulders. "I guess I am a little tired." Now he was lying to his son.

Zane strolled over to the black saddle and touched it. "Did Grandpa really use this saddle?"

"Yes, he did."

"Are you going to keep it forever?"

Zane was always full of questions and tonight Jude was just too tired to answer. Zane continued to walk around the room touching things. Something was different. His son wasn't happy, as he usually was when he returned from seeing his mother.

"What's wrong?"

"Nothing," Zane replied quickly again, and picked up an overstitch spacer tool and studied it.

Jude watched him for a moment and then asked again, "What's wrong, son?"

Zane made his way to Jude's desk and sat on

it, facing Jude. "It's nothing, really, but Mama is going back to California soon."

Fury slammed into his stomach unexpectedly. He'd been dreading this moment. Ever since Paige had returned, he'd been wondering when she'd leave. For he knew beyond a doubt that she would.

"How do you know this?"

"She got a phone call and she seemed upset and I asked her what was wrong. She said her time here was up and she would have to return to California soon."

"How did that make you feel?"

Zane shrugged. "I'm fine, Dad."

But he wasn't. Jude could see that. "When is she leaving?"

Zane shrugged again. "I don't know."

"You didn't ask?"

"No, Dad, I didn't ask. I'm cool with it. Really. She gave up so much to become a doctor and now she has to finish it. I understand that. I'll see her again."

Jude didn't get it. She should have told him before she told Zane. That was what made him angry. He got to his feet. "It's getting late. We better go to the house."

"But it's Saturday tomorrow and we can sleep late."

Jude ruffled his son's hair. "Since when? We still have hay to get off the ground tomorrow and I'll be up before the sun."

Zane jumped off the desk. "I can help. Uncle Elias said he was going to teach me to be tough."

"Oh, really." They went through the door and Jude closed it.

"Can I ride piggyback, Dad?"

That threw Jude. Zane was acting insecure, needing to be close to Jude. That meant he was upset and acting much younger than he was.

He was always telling everyone how big he was, but tonight he needed his dad.

Jude squatted and Zane climbed on and they made their way to the house. "How is Elias going to make you tough?"

"He said if I could pick up a bale of hay, I would get big muscles."

"You want big muscles?"

"Well, at the time I thought if I got stronger, the McCrays wouldn't pick on me anymore. But lately they've left me alone."

"Has Dudley said anything to you?"

"No, except one day I met him as I was going into my English class and he saw I wasn't on crutches anymore. I told him I was all healed and he nodded and walked away. He didn't say a word. I mean, I was the one who was whupped like an old coon dog who won't hunt. He could have said something."

His son was listening too much to Grandpa. Then, Jude had, too, at that age, even though

Grandpa's stories and sayings were 99 percent fiction and 1 percent truth. All the Rebel boys had grown up with those stories and Jude wouldn't change a thing about it.

"There are a lot of McCrays, Dad. And there's only one Rebel. That's me. We need more Rebels in school."

"Baby John will be in school by the time you graduate."

"Yeah, I guess it's just me for now."

A quarter moon hung high in the sky and the darkness of the night surrounded them as Jude made his way to the house. Crickets chirped a song he knew well and horses neighed in the pasture. All familiar sounds. Home. Jude never wanted to leave.

Zane rested his head next to Jude's and an all-powerful protective force filled Jude. He never wanted anyone to hurt his son again. He was still steaming that Paige had told Zane before she had told him. Surely she understood that Zane would be upset.

"Dad, I have a tiny scar on my forehead where you have a scar. In the exact same spot. And both wounds were inflicted by a McCray. Did it hurt when you were shot?"

"I don't remember, son. It was a long time ago." Jude was reeling too hard from his anger toward Paige to even think about that time. "Why are you asking about it?"

"I don't know. I don't understand why people can't live in peace."

Zane had said this several times and it genuinely bothered him when people fought. He was probably thinking about his parents fighting because there were going to be fireworks when he saw Paige. This time he wouldn't be silent.

Zane was quiet the rest of the way to the house, and once inside, his grandma had banana pudding waiting and he sat down and ate a bowlful. After that, Jude made him go to bed with a promise that he could help with the hay hauling tomorrow. After his son was sound asleep, he slipped downstairs and told his mom he was going out for a while in case Zane woke up. But he never did. He usually slept soundly.

Jude got in his truck and headed toward Paige's. Tonight he wouldn't accept any evasive answers. She was telling him exactly what she had planned and he would tell her if she could continue to see Zane or not. He hated that it had come to this. But she owed them more than a goodbye. A hell of a lot more.

JUDE DROVE INTO the driveway and noticed that the garage door was down but lights were on in the house. He walked to the front door and knocked. And waited. Frustrated, he knocked again.

"Paige, it's Jude," he called through the door.

"Just a minute!" she shouted back.

In a second the door opened and she stood there in nothing but a towel. She was drying her hair with another towel. The sight of her clean, smooth skin knocked all his rage sideways. But he recovered quickly.

He brushed past her into the kitchen, where the light was on, and turned to face her. "I trusted you not to hurt him."

"What?" She stopped drying her hair. "What are you talking about?"

"I'm talking about Zane. He's upset."

"About what? He was fine when I dropped him off at the house."

"You don't get it, do you? You just can't do that to a child."

Her eyes clouded with concern. "You'll have to explain what you're talking about."

"You told him you're leaving."

"Yes, and we talked about it. He seemed

fine. Are you saying he's upset because I'm leaving?"

"Yes. He says he's not, but I know my kid and he's pushing down all his feelings again. How could you do that to him? And how could you tell him before me? At least I could have been ready for the fallout."

She headed toward the hall. "I have to see him."

He caught her arm and wished he hadn't. Her smooth, satiny skin defused everything inside him but his need for her. With strength he didn't know he possessed, he removed his hand.

"No. I will take care of Zane and you will explain to me your plans and how you could hurt him like this. I don't want any evasive answers. I want to know your plans for the future concerning Zane."

"Okay." She tensed, her green eyes stormy. "Dr. Spencer called while Zane was here and explained my allotted time was up and I needed to return. I told her I would be in California on Monday. Zane asked me what was wrong because I was a little upset when I got off the phone. I told him that I had to go back for a couple of days to pack my things and explain to Dr. Spencer and the staff that I would be leaving. I promised him I would be back as soon as I could. Hopefully, not more than two days."

"What?" Jude was completely thrown and at a loss for words. "You're quitting at this stage?"

"I'm not spending any more time away from my son. Time is too valuable and I've missed too much. My career doesn't mean anything without him."

"You can't just give it up after all the work and the heartache."

"I don't plan on giving it up. I can finish later or work something out. I have to talk to Dr.

Spencer first to see what my future holds. But I know one thing for certain—my son comes first this time."

What about me? She always conveniently left him out.

"I either misunderstood Zane or…"

"Leaped to the wrong conclusion," she finished for him. "Do you think that badly of me?"

"I'm not thinking at all, it seems, just reacting."

She moved closer to him. "Jude, let's get it right this time. I think you know how I feel about you. After all these years, how do you feel about me?"

He looked into her green eyes and saw everything he'd ever wanted, but the doubts still lingered. But this time he had to speak up. He had to say what he was feeling and he had to say what he wanted. And he was adult enough now to handle her answer.

When he remained silent, she asked, "Are you still involved with the teacher?"

"No. That was nothing. Our interest was Zane and that was it. Even if you hadn't come back, it probably would have fizzled out."

"Why?"

Words crowded his throat and he had to say them. He'd never dreamed it would be this hard.

"Why, Jude?"

He cleared his throat. "Because there's only one girl for me. And always will be." He reached out and gently stroked her cheek with his thumb. "I love you."

"Oh, Jude. I've never stopped loving you, either. What are we going to do about it?"

He took her hand and held it, wanting to get it right. Years ago he'd gotten it so wrong, but now he wanted it to be perfect. "Will you marry me?"

Both hands covered her mouth and she started to cry. "Oh, oh…"

"Paige…"

She threw herself into his arms then and he held her so tight he could feel her heart beating against his. "Yes, yes, yes!"

His lips found hers and they got lost together in the magic of love, of finding each other again and enjoying all its rewards. When he could breathe again, he took her hand and led her to the bedroom.

He cradled her face in his hands. "I'm so glad that there's always this. Perfect. Harmony. Together." He punctuated each word with a kiss and then slowly removed the towel. They fell onto the bed, both laughing, both happy, both enjoying the maturity that the years had brought.

Jude pulled the teddy bear from beneath him. "You don't need this anymore."

"No. I now have the real thing."

A LONG TIME later Paige woke up in Jude's arms, and even though the sun wasn't out, it was shining bright in her heart. This time they connected on a level they both understood and she would never let this man down again. She would love him for the rest of her life.

He stirred and they shared a long kiss. "I don't like the thought of being away from you," he said. "Not even for a couple of days."

"Then come with me to California."

He stroked her tangled hair from her face. "I was thinking the same thing. I don't want you to stop the residency. I want you to finish it. I haven't had a vacation in years. I've taken Zane to NASA several times and to SeaWorld and Schlitterbahn. He has about two and a half weeks' more of school and I think if I talk to his teachers, they will just go ahead and pass him because his grades are so good."

"What are you saying?"

"Zane and I are going to California with you and stay until you finish your residency."

She buried her face in his neck, breathing in the scent of him, the essence of everything that was Jude. Her heart was so full she could barely talk. "You said you would never leave Rebel Ranch."

"I'm not leaving it forever. I'm taking a long vacation to be with a woman I love because I can't stand to be away from her anymore."

She raised her head to look into his eyes. Even though she couldn't see them in the darkened room, she could feel them. She could feel everything about him. Laying her head on his chest, she sighed with contentment and listened to his heartbeat.

Forgiving herself had come slowly, like a gentle rain of tears on her broken soul, seeping into the crevices and gradually reaching her frozen heart, nourishing and bathing it with renewed warmth until all the guilt and heartache was gone. She could now accept life for what it was and for what it had been. All because this wonderful man had given her back her life.

"Hey, Jude, I love you."

Epilogue

Three months later...

When the plane touched down in Austin, Texas, there were three happy Rebels on it. Jude was happier than he'd ever been, and the smiles on his wife's and son's faces reflected that feeling. They'd had a private bonding time and they'd become a family.

They had gotten married quickly, three days after Jude had proposed. Staci had wanted to handle the wedding and they'd let her. They were married by a minister in the hotel and the reception was there, too. It was small and private ceremony with just the family. And then they flew away on an adventure of a lifetime.

At first, Jude felt like a fish out of water in the city atmosphere. But he soon adjusted as he and Zane explored Berkeley, San Francisco, Oakland, San Diego and small towns along the Pacific coast. They went sailing, snorkeling and swimming and enjoyed the beach. Jude wore flip-flops and shorts and his whole body was getting tanned, as was Zane's. He also loved the cooler temperatures, but he wasn't crazy about the fog. When Paige had a couple of days off, they took trips to Disneyland and Hollywood. It was a vacation every day. And every day was perfect because they were together.

They lived in Ms. Whitman's house because she wasn't expecting new tenants until September. They had the run of the place because the lady had gone to visit her son and his family in Seattle. Jude liked the woman and he also liked Thea. They both were very warm and loving women and Jude was grateful that they had been there for Paige.

Even though they enjoyed sightseeing and exploring new places, their favorite time was when they went to the hospital with Paige. Zane loved going with his mother on rounds and just being in the atmosphere. Jude felt there would probably be another doctor in the family one day.

But Jude missed home. He missed the wide-open spaces, dirt beneath his feet and being on a horse. As long as he could wake up with Paige beside him and go to sleep with his arms around her, everything evened out.

While they'd been gone, a new Rebel had been born into the family. Egan and Rachel's baby son was now a week old and they couldn't wait to see him. His name was Justin.

Today was Zane's birthday and they'd made it home just in time. Their thirteen-year-old son ran ahead of them through the airport to the luggage carousel. Quincy and Jenny were picking them up. Jenny was now pregnant and there would be another Rebel in the family come March. Zane spotted them first and ran and jumped into Quincy's arms as if he was five years old. He'd missed his uncle.

"Hey, partner, happy birthday," Quincy said, still hugging his nephew. "I think you've grown a foot."

"Yeah. I'm getting tall like Dad."

Everyone hugged and then they started the trip home. Zane talked nonstop all the way about California and his mom and her job. Jude thought he might have to put a gag in his mouth, but it was nice to see his son so happy.

When they turned onto Rebel Road, Jude felt a lightness in his chest, and when he saw the cattle guard and the ranch, that sensation gave way to joy. He reached for Paige's hand.

He was home. They were home. And it had never felt so good.

They'd talked about where they would live, but to Zane there was only one place to live. With Grandma. That was home to him. Jude wasn't going to get past living with his mother, but one day he wanted them to have their own home.

Everyone was waiting, even Staci, when they reached the house, which was decorated with balloons, banners and streamers for Zane's birthday. After all the hugging and kissing and once they'd all held the new baby, everyone sang "Happy Birthday." The smile on Zane's face said it all.

Later, he and Paige strolled to the barn to watch their son ride Bear. They leaned on the fence and Zane raced off on the horse.

"We made it." Jude put an arm around his wife. "Tonight we'll move my bed into Falcon's old room. It's bigger and has a balcony and we'll have our own bath. Our son will have his own bath, too."

"Now real life begins."

Paige had several interviews with different medical practices in Austin and Temple. She still had to take the Medical Licensing Exam. That was all in front of them. And Jude had to kick it in high gear since he'd been away. His brothers were still finishing up hay season and he would now be working long days.

She looked up at him, her eyes shining as bright as Zane's. "But it's all worth it." She smoothed the fabric of his Western shirt. "I was thinking, and don't freak out, of having another baby."

He smiled. "That's not freaking me out. That's making my day. I'd love nothing more than to have another child with you. Together. To experience everything it's supposed to be. And this time we'll get it right."

She glanced toward their son in the distance.

"I think we got it right the first time. Just in a different way." She wrapped her arms around his neck. "I love you. Don't ever let me go again."

He didn't plan to. Ever.

* * * * *

MILLS & BOON®

Why shop at millsandboon.co.uk?

Each year, thousands of romance readers find their perfect read at millsandboon.co.uk. That's because we're passionate about bringing you the very best romantic fiction. Here are some of the advantages of shopping at www.millsandboon.co.uk:

* **Get new books first**—you'll be able to buy your favourite books one month before they hit the shops

* **Get exclusive discounts**—you'll also be able to buy our specially created monthly collections, with up to 50% off the RRP

* **Find your favourite authors**—latest news, interviews and new releases for all your favourite authors and series on our website, plus ideas for what to try next

* **Join in**—once you've bought your favourite books, don't forget to register with us to rate, review and join in the discussions

Visit **www.millsandboon.co.uk**
for all this and more today!